THIRTEEN MEANS MAGIC

"Hey, Dawn, look out!" Jennifer cried. The Frisbee whizzed past Dawn's head. She jumped up and tried to grab it, but it sailed into the trees behind her.

That's what you get for daydreaming about such silly things, Dawn told herself, going into the woods after the Frisbee. She scanned the area for the plastic saucer, but she didn't see it anywhere. Her eyebrow twitched with mild irritation.

Then it appeared. The moon-colored disk rose from the ground and spun upward, all on its own. Dawn gasped. This was no accident. She summoned up every ounce of courage she had and willed the Frisbee to come toward her. She raised her eyebrow slowly. A queasy feeling had settled in the pit of her stomach.

The saucer approached her, teetering slightly in its orbit. *Stop!* Dawn thought, adding the swift motion of her eyebrow. The Frisbee stopped in midair, spinning in place. She stared at it in wonder. Her body tingled. Her pulse raced. It was incredible. But it was true. There was no mistaking it this time.

She kept her gaze on the disk as it hung suspended in the fresh afternoon air. Dawn Powell, ordinary Crestfield mid⊔ ⊔⊔⊔ ⊔⊔⊔ turned thirteen. *And she ha⊔*

Other Bantam Skylark Books you will enjoy
Ask your bookseller for the books you have missed

THE LOVE POTION (Abracadabra #2) by Eve Becker
HORSE CRAZY (The Saddle Club #1) by Bonnie Bryant
HORSE SHY (The Saddle Club #2) by Bonnie Bryant
HORSE SENSE (The Saddle Club #3) by Bonnie Bryant
HORSE POWER (The Saddle Club #4) by Bonnie Bryant
GOING HOME by Nicholasa Mohr
HEY, DIDI DARLING by S.A. Kennedy
MAYBE NEXT YEAR . . . by Amy Hest
THE GREAT MOM SWAP by Betsy Haynes
THE GREAT BOYFRIEND TRAP by Betsy Haynes
MISSING by James Duffy
THE GHOST IN THE THIRD ROW by Bruce Coville
THE GHOST WORE GRAY by Bruce Coville

Abracadabra #1

Thirteen Means Magic

Eve Becker

A BANTAM SKYLARK BOOK®
NEW YORK · TORONTO · LONDON · SYDNEY · AUCKLAND

RL 5, 009–013

THIRTEEN MEANS MAGIC
A Bantam Skylark Book / October 1989

Skylark Books is a registered trademark of Bantam Books,
a division of Bantam Doubleday Dell Publishing Group, Inc.
Registered in U.S. Patent and Trademark Office and elsewhere.

Produced by Daniel Weiss Associates, Inc.,
27 West 20th Street, New York, NY 10011

Cover art by Michael McDermott

Abracadabra is a trademark of Daniel Weiss Associates, Inc.

ISBN 0-553-15730-2

Published simultaneously in the United States and Canada

Bantam Books are published by Bantam Books, a division of Bantam Doubleday Dell Publishing Group, Inc. Its trademark, consisting of the words
"Bantam Books" and the portrayal of a rooster, is Registered in U.S. Patent
and Trademark Office and in other countries. Marca Registrada. Bantam
Books, 666 Fifth Avenue, New York, New York 10103.

PRINTED IN THE UNITED STATES OF AMERICA

O   9 8 7 6 5 4 3 2 1

To Margot, Bill, and Clipper

One

BOOM! A bolt of lightning ripped through the morning sky and raindrops pounded against the windowpanes. Dawn Powell rubbed the sleep from her eyes and sat up in bed. She pushed aside the curtains and peered out at the storm. Normally a little bad weather wouldn't bother her. It was a good excuse to curl up with a book or to practice her guitar. But today was different. Today Dawn turned thirteen.

The refrigerator downstairs was filled with sandwiches, potato salad, pickles, and cole slaw, all waiting for the great birthday picnic Dawn had planned. How could it rain on such an important occasion? she wondered. It was supposed to have been a perfect August day. She had been dreaming about it for weeks now—the summer sun warming the water down at the old rock quarry, an occasional fluffy cloud drifting by. She sighed. Her left eyebrow arched sharply the way it always did when she felt particularly emotional.

At that moment, the dark sky was split by a shimmering ray of sunshine. Patches of blue sky appeared and pushed aside the blanket of gray. Within seconds, the storm had completely disappeared!

Dawn gasped. What had just happened was exactly the way she had pictured it, right down to the parade of cottony clouds floating across the sky. How could a day so dismal have cleared up in the time—well, in the time it took her to raise her eyebrow? It didn't seem possible.

Dawn opened the window wide, and a gentle breeze caressed her face. She was amazed at her good luck. What could be a better birthday present than this? As she leaned out the window to smell the fresh air, a current of excitement raced through her. This was going to be a very special year. Even the weather was on her side.

Dawn sat quietly on the grass, surrounded by her family and her friend Megan Stark, a big birthday cake in front of her. The sun felt warm on her back and shoulders. The water in the quarry rippled gently.

"Make a wish and blow out the candles," Dawn's cousin, Jennifer Nicholson, called out. She pointed to the candles flickering on top of the cake she had made. It was covered with purple frosting and the number 13 was outlined in red. Trust Jennifer to bake a really different birthday cake—a dessert that made you laugh, Dawn thought. Jennifer was like that. And it was one of the reasons she was Dawn's favorite cousin and very best friend in the whole world.

Dawn squeezed her eyes shut. What did she want to wish for most? She wouldn't have minded not towering over all the girls in her class, and most of the boys, too. Or maybe she should wish for a little more of a figure. As it was, she was all arms and legs. And it might be kind of fun to have beautiful blond curls like Jennifer, instead of such *medium* hair—medium brown, medium straight, medium long.

But those weren't the kinds of things you could change by blowing out birthday candles. Besides, wishes weren't supposed to be about looks. A really good wish had to be about something big and important.

Dawn held her breath and formed a sentence in her mind. *I wish for this birthday to be the start of something new and wonderful.* She opened her eyes and blew as hard as she could. The flames flickered and went out. Before Dawn could catch her breath, the candles began to spark again. In an instant, the flames sprang back to life.

Dawn blinked. What on earth was going on? Then she noticed her cousin trying to keep a straight face. "Jennifer!" Dawn shook her head and laughed. "Trick candles! I should have guessed."

"Want some help, sweetheart?" Her father leaned toward the cake.

Dawn nodded and she and her father blew as hard as they could. The flames died down and then flared up again. Laughter rang across the quarry as the candles sizzled right down to the bottom of their wicks and finally went out.

Dawn felt a pang of worry. "Does this mean my wish won't come true because I didn't actually blow out the candles?"

"Of course not, dear," her mother assured her. "It's the love and good wishes of the people around you who help make a birthday wish come true."

Jennifer caught Dawn's eye and clutched her heart in a theatrical gesture. Dawn let out a giggle.

"What did you wish?" piped up Paul, Dawn's eleven-year-old brother.

"If she tells you, it won't come true," Dawn's sister, April, said.

Paul made a face. "Just because you're the oldest doesn't mean you know everything. I don't care about her dumb old wish, anyway." He picked up a pebble and hurled it into the quarry.

"Brothers!" Megan whispered to Dawn. Megan had *two* of them, so she knew what they were like.

Megan and her family had just moved to Ohio from Michigan at the beginning of the summer, and Jennifer had gotten to know her right away. Then she'd introduced Megan to Dawn. That was the way things usually went. Jennifer was the out-going one. She met people first. But Dawn usually got to know them better. When Jennifer had gone off to camp for most of the month, Dawn and Megan had stayed in Crestfield and had become pretty good friends.

Jennifer had arrived home from camp just in time for Dawn's birthday. "Well, aren't you going to taste the cake?" she asked impatiently. "I can't wait till you see what color it is *inside*!"

Dawn took the knife her mother handed her and eased out the first piece. "Yikes! It's green!" she shrieked. "I'm afraid to ask what flavor it is."

"Would I make my dear cousin and best friend anything but her favorite kind of cake?" Jennifer asked.

"Chocolate?" Dawn slid the piece of brightly col-ored cake onto a paper plate. "You mean to tell me this purple and green thing is chocolate?"

"The wonders of food coloring," Jennifer ex-plained.

Dawn licked some of the frosting from her fin-gers. Sure enough, it was fudgy and delicious. She sighed contentedly.

Jennifer also had a grab bag of presents for

Dawn, each wrapped in different colored paper—a rubbery brontosaurus that grew twenty times its size when placed in water, a pair of sunglasses that made rainbows around everything you looked at, and a great pair of socks with little stars and moons all over them.

"I bought every single thing by mail," Jennifer said proudly. She was always ordering things from catalogs.

Megan gave Dawn a colorful cotton sweater, and April gave her a charm bracelet.

"April, thank you!" Dawn slipped the bracelet around her wrist and the charms jangled delicately. The nicest charms were a little silver guitar and a tiny book that actually opened. Even if she was boy crazy, April was a pretty great sister.

Dawn's last gift was a glow-in-the-dark Frisbee from Paul. He went off to play with it almost as soon as Dawn had unwrapped it.

She had gotten her present from her parents that morning. Her new ten-speed bike was in the garage, a shiny pink ribbon around its sky blue frame.

Dawn lay back happily on the sweet-smelling grass. Sunlight shone through the tree branches and made patterns on the worn picnic blanket. There wasn't a trace of the storm that had seemed so threatening this morning. Dawn still couldn't get over how strange that had been. As soon as she had thought of clear weather, it had appeared, almost as if she had had something to do with it.

"Hey, want to see this new dive I made up in camp?" Jennifer's voice broke into Dawn's thoughts. Dawn sat up. She watched her cousin grab onto the limb of a tree near the water's edge. Hoisting herself up, Jennifer climbed quickly to a thick branch that jutted out high over the quarry.

"I think I can do it from here," she called. She inched forward until she was over the water. Then she stood up, holding her arms out for balance.

"Jennifer, dear, you just finished your cake," Dawn's mother said. "I think you'd better wait a few minutes before you go in."

"Aw, Aunt Nona, just one dive, okay?"

"Jennifer . . ." Dawn's father echoed.

"But *my* dad says it's not true about eating and swimming," Jennifer protested.

"That may be true," Dawn's mother replied. "But while he's away, we're in charge. You know that." Jennifer's mother had died when Jennifer was

8

six. Jennifer lived with her father, an archaeology professor at the nearby state university. Right now Uncle Kenneth was off on another one of his trips, digging up old bones.

"Besides," Mr. Powell added, "you don't look too sturdy up there. I wouldn't want anything to happen to my favorite niece." He had a very special place in his heart for his sister's only daughter.

Jennifer managed to give a little hop and still keep her balance. "Look, Uncle Bob. I'm totally fine here." She jumped once more, to prove her point.

As Jennifer landed, Dawn heard a chilling crack. "Jen!" she screamed. The branch was splitting where it met the tree trunk. Jennifer began to slip. Dawn eyed the sharp rocks at the quarry's edge. Her heart pounded wildly. She felt Megan grab her arm.

"No!" Dawn yelled. If Jennifer fell, she was going to land right on those rocks. *Don't let the branch break!* she pleaded silently. *Jennifer, don't fall!* Dawn felt her eyebrow arch sharply.

The cracking sound stopped, and the branch held steady. Dawn held her breath, her body quivering as Jennifer struggled to regain her balance. Jennifer managed to scramble down to solid ground and Dawn went limp with relief.

But the second her cousin was safe, Dawn's relief dissolved in a flood of amazement. What on earth had saved her? Once the branch had started cracking it should have broken off completely under Jennifer's weight. Except . . . except that Dawn had willed it to stay firm. Was that possible? Or was it a coincidence—just like the sudden change in the weather that morning. A chill ran up Dawn's spine and made her shiver. The change in the weather had happened in exactly the same way! She had lifted her eyebrow and instantly the thing she was hoping for had occurred.

"I think I said something about that tree not looking too stable," Dawn's father's voice sounded a little shaky. "You were a very lucky girl, Jennifer. It's a miracle the branch didn't break off altogether." His words echoed Dawn's thoughts. But Dawn was beginning to wonder if there wasn't more to it than a simple miracle.

Jennifer looked pale despite her summer tan. Mrs. Powell got up and put her arm around her. "Let's do something nice and safe," she suggested.

"How about joining Paul for a game of Frisbee? Let's go, everyone. Dawn?"

"Huh?" Dawn tried to focus on what her mother was saying. Her heart was beating uncontrollably and her head spun. What if she really *had* saved Jennifer?

"Dawn?" Mrs. Powell said again. "Honey, you look more shaken up than Jennifer."

Dawn eyed the tree branch again. "It's just that Jen . . . well, she should have . . . I mean . . ."

"I know," her mother said gently. "But she was lucky. She's just fine now." It was true. The color had returned to Jennifer's cheeks and she looked completely relaxed.

Dawn swallowed hard. She didn't feel so fine. If she voiced what she was thinking, no one would believe her in a million years. She wasn't sure if she truly believed it, either. Maybe all the excitement of turning thirteen was giving her an overactive imagination. She took a few deep breaths. She had to get these ideas out of her head.

"So, how about it, birthday girl?" her father prodded.

Dawn managed a nod. She joined her brother

and the rest of the group on the sun-drenched stretch of grass that served as their playing field. But she couldn't keep her mind on the game. She kept thinking about the morning's storm and Jennifer's close call up in the tree.

"Hey, Dawn, look out!" Jennifer cried. The Frisbee whizzed past Dawn's head. She jumped up and tried to grab it, but it sailed into the trees behind her.

That's what you get for daydreaming about such silly things, Dawn told herself, going in after the Frisbee. Her feet sank into the blanket of pine needles and earth softened by the morning's downpour. She scanned the area for the plastic saucer, but she didn't see it anywhere. She went farther into the woods, then crouched down and looked under some bushes. Not there. Her eyebrow twitched with mild irritation.

And then it appeared. The moon-colored disk rose from the ground and spun upward, all on its own. It turned and flew toward her. Dawn put out her hands as if to drive back the whirling saucer. Her eyebrow went up again.

The Frisbee immediately changed course, steering away from her. Dawn gasped. This was no accident. She summoned up every ounce of courage she had and willed the Frisbee to come toward her. She raised her eyebrow slowly. A queasy feeling had settled in the pit of her stomach.

The saucer approached her again, teetering slightly in its orbit. *Stop*! Dawn thought, adding the swift motion of her eyebrow. The Frisbee stopped in mid-air, spinning in place. She stared at it in wonder. Her body tingled. Her pulse raced. It was incredible. But it was true. There was no mistaking it this time.

She kept her gaze on the disk as it hung suspended in the fresh afternoon air. Dawn Powell, ordinary Crestfield middle schooler, had just turned thirteen. *And she had magical powers!*

Two

"Hey, Dawn!"

Dawn whirled around at the sound of her cousin's voice. As she took her gaze off the Frisbee, it stopped spinning and dropped to the ground.

There was a flash of color between the trees. Jennifer stepped into view. "What are you doing?" she demanded.

Dawn's heart was beating so hard she could hear it pounding in her ears. She held her breath. Had Jennifer seen what had happened?

"You've been in here forever," Jennifer said. "Haven't you found that Frisbee yet?

Dawn let her breath out just a little. Jennifer hadn't seen anything.

"The Frisbee's right here," she said weakly. The glow-in-the-dark material shone ever so slightly in the shade of the trees. Dawn eyed it nervously. She half expected it to rise up and start flying around again.

"Well, why don't you pick it up?" Jennifer asked. "We can't exactly play without it, you know." She eyed her cousin more closely. "Hey, Dawn, what's wrong?"

"Wrong? Um, nothing's wrong," Dawn said slowly. That was true enough. You couldn't exactly say there was something wrong with having magical powers.

"Come on, Dawn. Tell me." Jennifer said. "We don't keep any secrets from each other, right?"

"Of course we don't," Dawn managed to say. "It's just that, well, Jen, something strange is going on." Dawn didn't quite know how she was going to explain something she couldn't believe herself. "I—I'm, um, different."

"Of course you are," Jennifer said matter-of-factly. "You're thirteen now." Jennifer had turned thirteen at the beginning of the summer and considered herself an expert. Then a note of excitement crept into her voice. "Isn't it great, Dawn? Finally we're *both* teenagers!"

"Great," Dawn echoed. But her mind was on her incredible discovery, not on what Jennifer was saying.

"Hey, you're not worried about starting eighth grade, are you?" Jennifer asked. "Because it's going to be the best. I mean, think of it! The eighth-graders practically run Crestfield Middle School."

Dawn nodded. There were plenty of reasons she'd been looking forward to school this year. For one thing, the eighth-graders always got the best solos in the school choir recitals. And the most space in the literary magazine. Dawn knew these weren't the things that Jennifer was referring to, but they were what mattered to her. Plus, everyone looked up to the eighth-graders. Maybe, just maybe, Dawn would feel a tiny bit less shy this year, and a tiny bit more outgoing. More like her cousin.

But in all her wildest dreams about eighth grade, Dawn had never imagined starting the new school year with magical powers. Suddenly, all the possibilities raced through her mind. Sunny, warm weather every day, even in the winter. Gourmet food in the cafeteria. No homework! But could Dawn really do all these things? Her questions about her new power mingled with a feeling of amazement. How had this happened to her?

What if Dawn really *could* make her dreams come true? What would the other kids at school think? One thing was certain. Once they knew she had magic powers, they'd treat her differently from everyone else. Dawn frowned. Maybe she wouldn't tell them.

Jennifer took her frown the wrong way. "Look, you don't have a single reason to worry about eighth grade," she said. "We both know you'll be on the honor roll, as usual. And you'll probably get one of those big parts in the choir you keep talking about, too. I mean, you're the smartest, most talented person in the whole school."

Dawn felt herself blushing. "That's only what you think. Gary Elwood's a lot smarter."

"That creep?" Jennifer dismissed him with a wave of her hand.

Dawn felt a little sorry for Gary. All his brains didn't make up for the teasing he took. He was teased constantly just because he was different. But not as different as a middle schooler with magical powers.

Now that Dawn was thinking about it, she *was* a little nervous about school. There was only one solution. Her magic would remain her own wonderful secret. *Nobody* would find out about it. Well, except Jennifer. But she wasn't going to tell Jennifer until she really knew what her powers could do. Dawn still half expected to wake up and find out that she had dreamed this entire day.

But she hoped not. Eighth grade by itself could be fun . . . Dawn stooped down to pick up the Frisbee. But eighth grade with magic could be absolutely amazing!

"And now for my encore!" Dawn announced to her imaginary audience late that afternoon. She couldn't help feeling a tingle of pride as she looked around her bedroom. She shared the room with April, and it was usually a disaster area. But now both beds were neatly made, their matching powder blue comforters spread over them perfectly. Her birthday presents were put away, and the new notebooks and supplies she and April had bought for school were stacked carefully on the long, wooden desk they both used. Even the poster that had been coming off the wall was back up securely. And all Dawn had done was arch one eyebrow.

The only messy spot left was her sister's dresser. The top of it was a jumble of creams and makeups, hair ribbons, and jewelry.

Dawn concentrated on a mental picture of order—the bottles and jars standing in a neat row, the lipsticks lined up next to the eyeshadows, the earrings and bracelets separated into compartments in the glass jewelry box. Her eyebrow shot up. The mess on the dresser grew wobbly and blurry, like a TV set gone out of focus. A split second later, April's things were all perfectly organized on her dresser top.

"Good job," Dawn congratulated herself. Was April going to be surprised when she got home! For the final touch, Dawn arched her eyebrow at the full-length mirror on the closet door. It was immediately sparkling clean with not a speck of dust on it.

Dawn smiled at her reflection. The face that smiled back at her was the same one she always saw when she looked in the mirror. Hazel eyes, straight nose—maybe a little too long—wide mouth, pale skin with a smattering of freckles. There wasn't a clue that she was any different than she'd been the day before. But she was. There was no question about it.

Dawn flopped down on the freshly made bed. She did have magical powers. She couldn't wait to see the look on her cousin's face when she told her. Jennifer was going to be absolutely thrilled. Dawn smiled as she thought about all the fun they would have together. They were going to have a terrific year, just as she had hoped. But as quickly as her excitement had come, it faded. Dawn felt a sting of nervousness. What if Jennifer thought *she* should have gotten magical powers instead? Or what if she thought Dawn was weird? Maybe she would think Dawn came from another planet.

Stop it! Dawn scolded herself. *Jennifer thinks it's great to be different. She'll be happy for you.* Suddenly she couldn't wait to tell her cousin.

Impulsively, she wiggled her eyebrow. The door opened up all by itself. The hall telephone came sailing toward her, its cord skimming along the blue rug. Dawn reached for it.

BRRING! She jumped at the sound.

21

What if Dawn had been thinking about Jennifer so hard that somehow, magically, she had gotten her to call? Dawn's stomach tightened. She stared at the phone as it settled onto the bed and rang again. Her hand trembled as she picked up the receiver. "Hello?"

"Hello, my dear," said a high-pitched, slightly creaky voice that was definitely not Jennifer's. "How is my very special granddaughter enjoying her birthday?"

"Grandma Cassie!" Dawn sank back happily against her pillows. She could picture her grandmother in the hot pink sweat suit she liked to wear for her afternoon meditation hour. Right now she was probably looking at Lake Erie out of the window of her cozy little house, having a cup of mint tea as she talked on the phone. Grandma Cassie wasn't one bit like the usual grandmother. And Dawn wouldn't have changed one single thing about her.

"Happy, happy birthday, Dawn," she said warmly. "It's a very special day, isn't it?"

"Definitely." *If you only knew,* Dawn thought.

"How are you celebrating this important birthday? Why aren't you out enjoying yourself?" Grandma chided lightly.

"Well, we had a picnic this afternoon," Dawn said. "It looked like we were going to get rained out, but then the weather suddenly cleared up." Dawn got a funny feeling inside as she thought about how she had changed the weather.

"Oh, I'll bet it did," Grandma said. "It just wouldn't do to let some bad weather get in the way of such a big event. I'm sure you took care of it right away."

Took care of it? Dawn giggled nervously.

"How does it feel to be thirteen, my dear? Tell me everything."

"Everything?" Dawn's voice came out in a squeak. She couldn't exactly tell her grandmother that she could make things fly around in the air. Even a grandmother as cool as Grandma Cassie. "Well, being thirteen is . . . different," Dawn managed.

"Oh, I know it is," her grandmother said. "I know all about it."

"You do? I mean how can you? I mean—I don't know what I mean." Dawn stumbled over her words.

"Dawn, dear, this may be hard for you to believe, but I turned thirteen once, too." Grandma Cassie said with a chuckle. "Just like you."

"Not just like me," Dawn blurted out. She was one of a kind—a very strange kind.

"Dawn, I understand," her grandmother said softly. Her voice was serious now. "I remember my thirteenth birthday. I didn't clear up a storm. I created one. A snowstorm. It was such a mild winter, you see, and I wanted to be able to go sleigh riding with my friends from town."

"You created a snowstorm?" Dawn wondered if she had heard right. "Grandma, that's impossible!"

"No more impossible than what you did."

"You mean you can do what I did?" Dawn asked.

"Yes, dear. It runs in the family."

Dawn's head was spinning. Her grandmother was magical, too? Everyone knew that Grandma Cassie was a little out of the ordinary, but still . . . this was almost more amazing to Dawn than finding out about her own powers. Then another incredible thought occurred to her. "Does Mom—" She couldn't seem to finish the sentence. "Or April—"

"No," Grandma Cassie said. "The trait skips a

24

generation. Some things do, you know. And even then, not everyone gets it. It's like any other inherited trait. You and Paul both look very much like your mother, while April got her fair coloring and bone structure from your father. That's called genetics. The study of genes."

"So I'm not the only one!"

"No, you're not. But there are very few of us in the family," Grandma Cassie said. "For example, your mother, my own daughter, has no idea. Very few people are as lucky as we are."

Dawn tried to digest what her grandmother was saying. She had magical powers because they ran in her family. She had inherited them, just as she had inherited her brown hair and freckles. "Grandma, I don't understand. How did this happen? Why me?"

"Very simple," Grandma Cassie replied. "Our special talent is due to syzygy."

"Syzy-what!?"

"Syzygy. It's when the sun, the earth and the moon all line up," her grandmother went on. "It's a very rare phenomenon that disturbs the forces of gravity." She said this as if it were all perfectly logical. "Do you understand?"

"Well, sort of. We learned about gravity in

school. But what does that have to do with my power?"

"We have a family legend—those of us with the power," she added. Dawn felt a surge of pride. She was a member of a very special part of her family.

"The legend tells of an ancestor who was born at precisely the strongest moment of this phenomenon," her grandmother explained. "At precisely that moment there was a severe electrical storm and a meteorite shower that disrupted the earth's magnetic field."

Dawn wrinkled her brow. She was trying hard to understand Grandma Cassie's explanation, but it sounded like a lecture in advanced science.

"I'll tell you what it means in plain English. It means that Newbert Charles Caldwell, my many-times great-grandfather, your—well, why bother with technicalities?—our relative came into this world at the precise moment when all the earth's forces were in a state of complete disruption—the split second when the laws of science didn't apply. He later discovered he had the power to disrupt those laws at will—a power that was passed down through the generations. To us, my dear."

Dawn nodded slowly, even though Grandma

Cassie couldn't see her. Or maybe she could. At this point, Dawn didn't know *what* her grandmother was able to do. Come to think of it, how had she found out about Dawn, anyway? "Grandma, how did you know I'm magical, too?"

"It's that funny little habit you have, dear. With your eyebrow. We all have it."

"Of course!" Now it made sense. Grandma had it, and Paul—"My stars!" Dawn whispered. "Paul does that, too! Grandma, do you mean to tell me that little pest can . . ." She trailed off in disbelief.

"No, dear. Not yet," her grandmother said. "The powers don't develop until one's thirteenth birthday."

Dawn felt a little better. At least she had another two years before she had to worry about what Paul would do with magical powers. "Why does it happen when you turn thirteen, Grandma Cassie?"

"Well, that's when you're beginning to mature in many ways. At thirteen you're old enough to use your special talent wisely. It's a big responsibility, you know."

Dawn gulped. "Responsibility?" So far, she'd only been thinking of the fun part.

"Don't sound so worried, my dear. There are

times to use the powers and times not to use the powers. You'll soon learn the difference. And you have to give your powers a rest from time to time. Otherwise, strange things can happen."

"What kinds of strange things?" asked Dawn.

"Well, your powers can get tired, just like any other part of you. And then they won't work properly for some time. What I'm telling you, you see, is not to depend on your magic too much. You're a sensible girl, Dawn. You'll be careful. And I know you'll never use your powers to do mean or frivolous things, so there isn't anything to worry about."

"Frivolous things? Does that mean I shouldn't use my powers for just any old thing?" Dawn asked. "You mean I shouldn't use them to change the lunch menu at school every day, or get out of a tough homework assignment?"

"Something like that."

"Oh." *So much for those plans,* Dawn thought.

"Although I suppose an occasional good school lunch or just-for-fun wish wouldn't upset the balance too much," her grandmother added.

"Oh, and one more thing," Grandma Cassie said. "Enjoy yourself, my darling. You'll find that this is the most marvelous birthday gift in the world. It's the beginning of something new and wonderful!"

Dawn felt a current of excitement race through her. Where had she heard those words before? Her own birthday wish! Grandma Cassie's words echoed what Dawn had wished for when she had tried to blow out her birthday candles. Well, it certainly looked as if she was going to get her wish. And a whole lot more, too.

Three

"Why, dah-ling, I'd *love* to dance," Dawn drawled. Her feather boa swirled around her shoulders as she waltzed across her bedroom. She tried not to step on the hem of her rose satin ball gown, but it was difficult in her sparkling, spike-heeled slippers.

She raised her eyebrow and the shoes were gone. Her bare feet sank comfortably into the rug. Mmm. That was better. Now she could really move to the violin music that came out of nowhere.

One, two, three, one, two, three. Dawn stepped in time to the music. Suddenly she spoke aloud.

"Okay, now for a fast song!" After a moment's thought, she recited a little rhyme:

> Satin and glitter
> And elegant sights
> Give way to loud music
> And rock 'n' roll nights!

Ever since Dawn had been a little girl, she had enjoyed making up poems. The day before, Grandma Cassie had suggested that poetry might sometimes come in handy for focusing her powers. She arched her eyebrow. Her long dress was instantly transformed into a pair of wild, leopard-print tights and an oversized black T-shirt. The faint melody of violin strings suddenly exploded into the fast, furious rhythm of electric guitars.

"Rock lives!" Dawn sang out, dancing wildly. All she needed to complete the picture was the studded leather bracelet on April's dresser. Her gaze lingered on it. She raised her eyebrow and willed it toward her. She moved it to the right, then to the left. She made it slow down and then speed up again. When the bracelet hovered close to her, she snatched it out of the air and fastened it on to her wrist.

Not bad, she told herself. After an afternoon of practice, she was getting better at controlling her powers. She spun to the music, shaking her shoulders and tossing her head. If only doing her homework could be as much fun as giving herself a lesson in performing magic.

When the song was over Dawn flopped down on her bed. Right now, she felt like having a Swiss cheese sandwich and a big glass of milk. She arched her eyebrow.

All that materialized was a glass of chalky-looking yellow liquid. Dawn sniffed it and took a tentative sip. Yuck! It was cheese-flavored milk! She put it down on the rug. Maybe she hadn't thought out her spell precisely enough.

> *A glass of cold milk*
> *And a good sandwich, please,*
> *Instead of this drink*
> *In the flavor of cheese.*

At first, nothing happened. Then the glass began to disintegrate right in front of Dawn's eyes. The liquid inside it poured onto the carpet. Dawn arched her eyebrow. But the cheese-flavored milk just seeped deeper into the rug.

Suddenly, she remembered what Grandma Cassie had said. Her powers could get exhausted if she used them too much. Dawn watched the stain forming at her feet. Her magic lesson was over. Her powers had vanished with that glass. She was aware of an empty ache in the pit of her stomach. It felt as if a special new friend had just disappeared.

"And right, glide, left, glide, push off and—darn!" Jennifer went into a spin on her roller skates only to collapse in a heap in the middle of Dawn's driveway.

"Jen, are you okay?" Dawn skated over quickly.

Jennifer picked herself up, and brushed the dirt off her polka-dotted boxer shorts. "I'm okay. All that's hurt is my ego." She stamped a skate against the blacktop. "Why can't I learn how to do this one simple turn?"

"Simple? Jen, the guy who showed us all those tricks was the freestyle champion of Ohio!"

"Well, I'm not trying to do a quadruple like he did. I just want to do one turn. Besides, Kitty can do it." Kitty was Jennifer's best friend—after Dawn—and the best girl athlete at Crestfield Middle School. Jennifer ran a close second when it came to gymnastics and skating.

"Jen, why don't you take a break?" Dawn suggested. "Making yourself black and blue isn't going to help."

"I don't have time for a break," Jennifer said stubbornly. "I made up my mind that I would get this trick figured out before school started."

Dawn could sympathize with Jennifer. On her birthday, Dawn had been sure she was going to start school with magical powers. Now she wasn't so certain. Her grandmother had told her not to worry, though. Her magic would be back within a couple of days. But it had been two days already and so far, no luck.

Jennifer skated up the driveway again, crossed her right skate in front of her left one, and went into the preparation for her turn. Dawn held her breath. Jennifer twirled halfway around. But as she pushed her left skate forward to complete the spin, one leg buckled and she fell forward onto her knee. Dawn could see an ugly line of red trickling down Jennifer's shin.

"Oh, Jen!" She skated over to help her cousin up.

Jennifer waved her away. "Thanks, Dawn, but I'm fine. It's nothing. Really." She dabbed at her knee with the bottom of her T-shirt, and stood up for another try.

"Maybe you should go in and wash that cut," Dawn suggested.

"No way." Jennifer was skating forward already. "I'm not going in until I can do this."

Dawn admired her cousin's determination, but maybe she was taking this skating thing too far. In a way, Dawn blamed it on her own parents. If their video company wasn't doing a series on young champions, Jennifer would never have met the skater who had shown her this complicated turn. For Dawn it was enough to master going backward and forward, but Jennifer wasn't content with anything less than a traffic-stopping trick.

Jennifer pushed her right leg forward. *If only I could help her,* Dawn thought. She arched her eyebrow just in case her powers were back. Jennifer got halfway around. Her left leg moved forward. Suddenly, her body whipped around. Not just once, but twice. And then an extra final half turn.

"I did it!" Jennifer bounced up and down—as close as she could come to jumping on her skates.

Dawn bounced up and down with her. *And I did it, too!* she echoed silently. *My powers are back!*

Jennifer skated forward and did one more graceful turn. Not a double, but Dawn hadn't had to help her this time, either. Then she glided backward, and stopped right in front of Dawn. "You're the best cousin in the whole world," she said. "I know I couldn't have done it without your help."

"You know?" Dawn heard her voice coming out in a little squeak.

"Well, sure. Everybody needs someone to cheer them on," Jennifer said matter-of-factly. "You gave me that extra ounce of determination."

"Determination. Right," Dawn said, trying not to laugh.

"Now it's your turn," Jennifer said.

"My turn?" Dawn shook her head. "Forget it, Jen. One acrobat on skates is enough."

"Aw, come on. Don't you want to start school tomorrow with a new trick you can show people!"

Now Dawn couldn't hold back an enormous smile. "That's okay, Jen. You're the trickster." *Besides, I have a few tricks up my sleeve already.*

Four

Dawn stood at the trelliswork gate in front of Jennifer's rambling old house on the first day of school. She took a step back and arched her right eyebrow sharply. The latch clicked up and the gate swung open. Dawn passed through, and it closed gently behind her. "Look, Ma, no hands," she said with a giggle.

Then she grew serious. *That's it for your magic for today.* she reminded herself silently. *Don't want to overdo it again.*

Dawn went up the walk and rang the Nicholsons' doorbell. While she waited for Jennifer to come to the door, she felt a little pang of guilt. She still hadn't gotten around to telling Jennifer what she'd discovered about herself.

Her problem faded from her thoughts as Jennifer opened the door and struck an exaggerated fashion model pose. "Tah-dah! Get ready, world! Here I come," she announced. She turned to give Dawn a complete view of her outfit.

"Wow, Jen, you look great!" Dawn said. Her cousin had on a black miniskirt topped by a bright red cropped cotton shirt. Her red hightops matched the combs in her curly blond hair perfectly. Jennifer really knew how to dress. Of course, she'd had to add a pair of plastic kids' sunglasses with Donald Duck on them. Just for laughs.

But then, Jennifer could afford to call attention to herself. Dawn was tall enough to be mistaken for a stop sign if she wore an outfit like that. And the sunglasses—well, she couldn't imagine wearing glasses like that to school.

Dawn was wearing a simple blue and white striped boating T-shirt to go with her jeans and tennis shoes. Her shoulder-length brown hair was tied back with a plain blue ribbon. She'd been satisfied with her outfit when she left home. But looking at Jennifer, she began to feel like Miss Wallflower.

"Dawn, don't you want to wear something—well, more special for the first day of school?"

Dawn felt a blush creeping across her face. "Really boring, huh?"

"Well . . . no. Of course not. They'd probably call your look 'classic' in *Seventeen*," Jennifer said. "It's just that you dressed the same way last year. We're the most important kids in school now. Don't you want to look a little different?"

Different? Dawn bit her lip. If only Jennifer had seen her dancing around her bedroom in those leopard-print pants a few days ago. But Dawn would never have the nerve to wear something like that to school. She was different enough already. Jennifer just didn't know it yet.

Jennifer went on. "Maybe if you rolled up the bottom of your jeans and borrowed my clip-on hoop earrings . . ." She eyed Dawn critically.

"Jen, you know that Mom doesn't let me wear big earrings to school yet. Besides, I wouldn't feel comfortable with a new look, anyway. Your style is great—for you, not me."

Jennifer shrugged. "I know you're just being shy. I guess it's none of my business, anyway. I just want everyone to notice you and know how terrific you are." She pulled the front door shut behind her and slung her backpack over one shoulder. Then she and Dawn headed back down the walk.

"I appreciate it," Dawn said. "And you're probably right. I am too shy. I guess I'm just never going to be Queen of the Lunchroom." She tried to make a joke out of it. "I'll leave that to you."

Jennifer waved her arm. "Sure, it may be kind of fun, but you don't get *A*'s from your teachers for that. I'd trade some popularity any day for a little of your magic in school."

Dawn froze. "Magic?" she squeaked.

"I mean, getting such good grades and being able to write poetry and everything. It seems sort of like magic to me."

"Oh." Dawn hoped Jennifer hadn't noticed her reaction. She took a few deep breaths and calmed down.

As she and Jennifer passed the town square, Dawn was surprised that it looked exactly as it had all summer long. Somehow, she expected everything around her to be a little different now. But the same brick walkways still crisscrossed the grassy lawn, and the wooden gazebo stood as it always did in the center of the square. On the other side the stores of downtown Crestfield were opening for the day as they always did at this hour.

"Well, maybe you'll get really good grades this year," Dawn said finally. "And I'll be less shy."

"And you'll get a big part in the choir concert, and I'll be the lead in the school play—especially if it's a comedy," Jennifer added.

"I hope." For a moment Dawn thought about casting a spell. It would be great to know these things would definitely happen. But then she remembered what her grandmother had told her about using her powers frivolously. It wouldn't be right to get everything she wanted the easy way.

She and Jennifer turned the corner. Crestfield Middle School came into view. The sight of the long, low building made Dawn's heart skip. This was it. This was eighth grade. And it was going to be special enough. Magic or not.

Oh, no! Barbie Davison's hand was waving around madly. Dawn groaned inwardly. *And I thought things were going to be different this year,* she thought. Some things never changed. Barbie *always* had to make herself the center of attention.

Of course, she did it with a smile on her face. And a lot of people seemed to fall for her act because of that.

Dawn had been taken in, too, for a while. Barbie always seemed to have something nice to say about Dawn's new pants or her history essay. And she had been nothing but encouragement when Jennifer had tried out for the girls' volleyball team.

Then Dawn had overheard her in the bathroom talking to Donna Lee. "Oh, Donna, I'm just positive you'll beat out Jennifer Nicholson for that spot on the volleyball team," Barbie had said.

In the end, one of the team players had gotten injured and the coach had taken both Jennifer and Donna. But ever since then, Dawn had noticed things about Barbie Davison that weren't very nice. For instance, when Barbie told Janie Simon she was sorry Janie had been absent from school, what she was really thinking was, "I'll just die if I don't find out where you were yesterday." When she said, "Let's get together Saturday," what she meant was, "Why didn't you invite me to the slumber party you're having this weekend?" Dawn kept trying to like Barbie. But it was difficult.

"Yes, Barbara?" Ms. Davenport said. Ms. Davenport was wearing her hair differently this year, and she looked prettier than ever. She was one of the best teachers at school and Dawn was glad to have gotten her for English.

Barbie put on her hundred-watt smile. "Well, I was thinking it might be fun if we read our compositions out loud. Then we could share our summers with each other. Wouldn't that be great?"

Dawn had a feeling that Barbie was just being nosy. As usual.

"We'll have to see, Barbara," Ms. Davenport answered. "Your suggestion would be fine if the assignment were simply to write about your summer vacations. But choosing the most emotional thing that happened is different. I'm trying to get you to describe happiness, or sadness, or excitement, or disappointment. Not just events. Do you understand? And some of that may be a bit personal to read aloud."

"But, Ms. Davenport, it's good to share secrets sometimes. We would all get a chance to know each other so much better."

Brother! This was supposed to be an English class—not a game of Truth or Dare. Dawn caught Jennifer's eye across the aisle. Jennifer twisted up her face as if she couldn't stand to listen to another word Barbie had to say. Dawn stifled a giggle.

"Barbara, perhaps you should concentrate on getting your own assignment written," Ms. Davenport suggested.

"Oh, it's all done." Barbie tossed her blond hair and looked pleased with herself. "I wrote about how exciting it was to be picked as the Toasties cereal girl." Barbie picked up her notebook as if she was about to start reading her composition.

"Bet she doesn't mention that her father *owns* Toasties cereal," Jennifer whispered across the aisle, loud enough for Barbie to hear.

Barbie just gave Jennifer a sticky-sweet smile and cleared her throat. "The Most Exciting Part of My Summer," she announced.

Dawn shook her head. Crestfield Middle School would definitely be better off if Barbie Davison woke up one day speaking nothing but Pig Latin.

And then Dawn got an idea. A wild idea. Grandma *had* warned her about using her powers in a mean way. Still, she didn't really think it was mean to teach Barbie a little lesson.

"Imagine having your face in every supermarket in America." As Barbie read, she seemed to glow at the idea of spreading her wonderful self around to every corner of the country.

Dawn couldn't resist for another minute.

> *Praising herself*
> *Is what Barbie does best,*
> *So make her speak Pig Latin*
> *And give us a rest.*

She whispered the poem under her breath and arched one eyebrow sharply.

"At's-thay at-whay appened-hay . . ." Barbie stopped talking abruptly and put her hand over her mouth. Then she tried again. "At's-thay at-whay . . ." She stopped again. Dawn could hear titters of laughter spreading through the room. Barbie's cheeks were coloring with embarrassment. The classroom erupted in noise and giggles.

"Class!" Ms. Davenport clapped her hands for attention. "Quiet down." Her voice was stern, but

Dawn thought she detected a glimmer of amusement in her teacher's eyes. "I think it's time to get to work," she shouted above the racket.

Everyone finally settled down, and the class continued. Silently reciting another poem Dawn took the spell off Barbie. But a few minutes of magic had clearly been more than enough for the Toasties cereal girl. No one heard a sound out of Barbie Davison for the rest of the period.

"Can you picture it?" Megan pushed her lunch tray through the cafeteria line. "You and me singing in front of the whole school and half the town!" Her red ponytail bobbed up and down as she talked.

Dawn inspected a plate of chicken. It was burned and dry-looking. She put it back and took the ravioli drowning in tomato sauce instead. Definitely not a gourmet meal. But it looked safer than the chicken. "Hold on, Megan. We haven't even auditioned yet."

"I know. But we'll work really hard, right? We'll sing the best audition Mrs. Renzulli has ever heard." Megan helped herself to some pudding that Dawn couldn't identify. She remembered her grandmother saying that a good meal at school once in a while wouldn't hurt. But she had already cast a spell on Barbie Davison, which was one spell more than she'd planned on casting that day.

"I'm definitely going to sing the best audition I can," Dawn said to Megan. She selected an apple that didn't look too bruised. Then she picked up her tray and glanced around the lunchroom.

Kids seemed to be sitting in the same spots as last year. The girls' cheering squad held court in one corner, and next to them sat the jocks. Dawn's friend Danny Page was at that table. Or rather, her ex-friend. She and Danny had grown up on the same block and had always played together when they were little. But since Danny had discovered football, he couldn't be bothered with anything else. Dawn sort of missed him.

Gary Elwood sat alone, punching buttons on his pocket calculator. Dawn felt a twinge of sympathy for him. She wondered if he felt lonely.

There were a few new faces around the lunchroom, too. One of them was her own brother's. Paul had already discovered where the jocks sat, and he and his friends from his old elementary school were occupying the nearest table possible.

Dawn caught Paul's eye and waved. He gave only the merest hint of a wave back. It was clear that he intended to assert his independence.

Dawn spotted Jennifer sitting at a table in the middle of the big, noisy room. Next to her was Kitty DeVries, in her Cleveland Indians cap. Last year she'd worn it with the brim in back. This year, Dawn noticed, she had it pulled down low over her short, dark hair.

Sue Flagg and Cindy Mitchell were sitting with Jennifer, too. Dawn thought Sue and Cindy were kind of stuck up. Cindy wore two watches. The blue one told what time it was in Crestfield. The red and black one was set on French time, just to remind everyone that Cindy had spent a winter vacation there once. Dawn found it hard to believe that Cindy had gone anywhere without Sue. They did everything together. They'd even gotten the same shoulder-length haircut with bangs for school this year. Sue and Cindy were part of the really popular crowd. And right now, all their attention was on Jennifer.

Jennifer's arms were up and she was making a hand over hand motion as if she were climbing. Then she pressed her palms together over her head

50

in a diving position. Dawn could see everyone at her cousin's table burst into laughter.

Dawn felt a tug of surprise as she realized that Jennifer was recounting what had happened to her at the picnic. And she felt a twinge of envy, too. It had been one of the scariest moments she could remember. But somehow Jennifer was making it hysterically funny! No wonder the most popular kids in school wanted to be friends with her.

As Dawn and Megan carried their trays over, Jennifer spotted them. "Hey, guys! I was just telling everybody about my miraculous escape from the quarry of no return!"

Dawn put her tray down. *If Jennifer only knew.* She was going to have to level with her cousin. And soon. But she couldn't very well do it in front of all these people. She decided she would have to have a heart-to-heart with Jennifer after school. When it was just the two of them, she would share her big news.

Her mind made up, Dawn slid into a seat. "Hi, everyone. This is Megan Stark. She moved here from Michigan this summer."

"Oh, hi. I recognize you from the tennis courts by Falcon Rock," Kitty said, peering out from under her baseball cap. "Welcome to Crestfield Middle School."

"Hi," Sue and Cindy echoed, almost in unison. But it was clear that they were more interested in Jennifer. They turned their attention back to her immediately.

"Hey, Jen, did I tell you I'm going back to France this Christmas?" Cindy asked. She tapped the red and black watch. *As if anyone needs reminding,* Dawn thought.

"Again?" Jennifer exclaimed. Dawn heard a note of jealousy in her cousin's voice. "Boy, some people have all the luck. Some of us have to stick around boring old Crestfield all year."

Dawn wondered how Jennifer was going to take *her* news.

Cindy seemed to lap up Jennifer's envy. "Well, not everyone's family has friends who live right down the street from the Eiffel Tower," she bragged. "I'll get to practice my French with their cute son, too."

"Hey, speaking of languages, I heard this rumor," Sue put in. "Someone told me that Barbie Davison started speaking Pig Latin in the middle of English class today."

"She did! It was wild!" Jennifer said. "All of a sudden, her words started coming out all jumbled up." Jennifer took a sip of milk. "I don't know, maybe she was just doing it for attention, but I had this really weird feeling that she couldn't control it. Know what I mean? It was as if someone had put a spell on her."

Dawn could feel her face growing hot. She busied herself by pushing her ravioli around in little circles with her fork. She couldn't look at her cousin.

"That's weird," Sue said.

"Are you sure you're not making up another one of your stories?" Cindy asked.

"No way. It really happened. Ask Dawn. She was there."

Dawn's fork fell out of her grip with a noisy clatter. "Yeah, um, it's true." She really wished someone would change the subject.

Kitty played with the brim of her cap. "What do you suppose made her do it?"

Jennifer put on her scary face and started humming the music from *The Twilight Zone*. Everyone laughed.

Except Dawn. *That's me,* she thought. *Dawn from*

the Twilight Zone. Weird. Scary. Different. If Jennifer's friends knew the truth about her, they'd probably clear out faster than you could say *abracadabra.* Of course, if it were Jennifer, she'd probably manage to wind up even more popular than she already was.

"Hey, Jen," Dawn heard Cindy say. "Sue and I are having a beginning of school slumber party this weekend. You can come, right?"

Jennifer leaned across the table and poked Dawn's shoulder. "I don't know. What are we doing this weekend? Can we go to Cindy and Sue's party?"

Dawn felt a sting of embarrassment. It was clear to her that the invitation was meant for her cousin. Yet Jennifer had assumed it was for both of them. "Well, uh, I guess it's okay. That is if Cindy and Sue want me to come." She kept her gaze down, studying the mess on her plate.

"Oh, sure you're invited," Cindy said hastily. "You too, Megan."

Once again, Dawn felt she'd been invited somewhere because of her cousin. Some time, she'd like to know how it felt to be really popular all on her own. Even more popular than Cindy or Sue. Or Jennifer. She pictured herself surrounded by people who hung on her every word, just as her cousin was now. It would feel so good to be accepted no matter what.

Oh my stars! Dawn realized she had accidentally arched her eyebrow. She had been so involved in her daydream that she forgot to control her old habit.

Before she knew what was happening, Cindy was talking to her eagerly. "Then it's all settled. You're definitely coming this weekend." She reached past Jennifer to give Dawn's arm a squeeze. "Great! I can't wait to hear all about your summer. Did you write any more poems like the ones you had in the literary magazine last year?"

Dawn couldn't believe what she was hearing. Since when was Cindy interested in her poetry? Last year, she'd gone around saying that the "lit-ah-rary" magazine was like one huge homework assignment.

Jennifer looked pretty surprised, too. And even Cindy herself wore a confused expression, as if she couldn't quite understand her own words.

Dawn forced herself to keep from laughing. She felt a bit odd. Still, she had to admit that it was nice to feel like part of the group.

But what had happened to her magic-free day? This was the second time she'd used her powers since school started. True, just now she hadn't done it on purpose. But maybe she owed it to herself to take back the spell.

"Hey, Dawn, wait until you see Jennifer's pictures from camp." Kitty's words cut into her thoughts. "It's really too bad you didn't come with us this summer."

Once more, Dawn felt a happy, warm rush of belonging. On second thought, maybe it wasn't such a great idea to revoke her spell.

"Hi, Dawn! How was your summer?" a familiar voice called. Dawn twisted around to see Danny Page walking by her table. His sandy hair curled at the collar of his sweatshirt. The smile in his blue eyes was directed right at her.

That did it. It wouldn't hurt to try a little popularity on for size. Just for a day or two. Just to know how Jennifer must feel. After all, what was the point of having magic powers if you couldn't use them?

Five

"Hey, Dawn!" Sue Flagg ran down the hall to catch up with her. "Listen, if you want to come over before Cindy's party this weekend, we can walk there together, okay?"

"Hi, Dawn," Wendy Hiller said as she passed by. "How was your summer? You look great."

Dawn felt a ripple of pleasure. The first day of school was always fun. But today went beyond anything she would have dreamed of a few weeks earlier. Suddenly, in the arch of an eyebrow, changing classes had gotten to be a lot like going to a big party. Maybe the music and the punch were missing, but the company sure wasn't.

Dawn attempted to answer both Sue and Wendy. "Thanks, Sue. Maybe I will walk to Cindy's with you. My summer was good, Wendy. You look nice, too."

"Hi, Dawn. My mom baked these Tollhouse cookies for my first day of school. Want one?" offered Liza Martin. "Here. This one's the biggest. And take another one if you want."

"Dawn, you're coming to our first basketball game of the year, aren't you?" Evan Thompson asked, coming up next to Liza. "We're playing the Sandusky Steamers."

"Definitely, Evan. Thank you, Liza," Dawn answered happily. Suddenly every person who passed her was a brand new friend.

"Hi, Dawn," a timid voice said.

Dawn turned to see Amy Page, a pint-sized version of her brother Danny, with a couple of friends.

"Hi, Amy. How's your first day at the middle school so far?" Dawn asked.

Amy giggled nervously. "Kind of fun and scary all at the same time. It's hard to get used to having every class in a different room with a different teacher."

Dawn smiled. Amy made her feel like an old pro. "Everyone feels that way at first. You'll get used to it."

"I suppose," Amy said. "Well, I'd better go." She carefully studied the schedule taped to the cover of her loose-leaf notebook. "I have to get to science now. Room 204."

"Mr. Everly? His classroom's right upstairs. And good luck." Mr. Everly was the strictest. Sixth-graders were always terrified of him.

Dawn watched Amy and her friends walk away. Seeing them reminded her of her own first day at the middle school. Lots of kids from Dawn's elementary school had started along with her, but she had still felt shy and lost. That day seemed as though it was a world away from today.

"That's Dawn Powell, isn't it?" Dawn heard one of Amy's friends say as they went down the hall.

"How do you know her?" the other one asked, a note of awe in her voice.

Was it that she was an eighth-grader, or was it her spell, Dawn wondered. She got to her locker and spun the dial, trying to memorize her new combination. As she pulled open the locker door, she heard a nasal voice behind her. "I noticed you're in accelerated math this year."

Dawn whirled around. Gary Elwood! After all the attention this afternoon, she was beginning to have more confidence in her powers. But this was absolutely incredible. In his entire career at Crestfield Middle School, Gary had never, ever been known to say a single word to any girl. His head was down and he shifted his weight uneasily. He was clearly embarrassed about this new experience, but he was urged on, just the same, by something that was totally out of his control.

Dawn felt guilty. She hadn't wanted to make anyone uncomfortable. "Yes, we're in the same math class this year, Gary," she replied. She waited patiently to see what else he would say.

He scuffed the toe of his sturdy lace-up shoe against the floor. His pants were too short and his white socks stuck out beneath the cuffs. Then he brightened. "I worked out a new equation at lunch today."

Dawn nodded. "That's nice, Gary," she said warmly.

"Maybe I could explain it to you sometime," Gary said. He fiddled with his plastic shirt pocket protector that held several pens and mechanical pencils.

Dawn didn't know what to say. Working on math problems with Gary wasn't really her idea of a fun afternoon, but he looked so hopeful. She didn't want to hurt his feelings. "Sure. Maybe sometime, Gary. Right now I'm about to be late for class, though." Dawn grabbed her books and banged her locker shut. "See you soon, okay?"

"Okay," Gary managed nervously.

Dawn gave Gary a smile and hurried away. As she glanced back, Gary was still rooted to the spot. He probably couldn't believe that he had just had his first conversation with a girl.

"Good grief, Dawn!" Barbie Davison seemed to swoop down out of nowhere. "Did I actually see Gary Elwood talking to you?"

It was incredible. Barbie didn't miss a thing. "Yes, Barbie, I guess you did."

"Well, I wouldn't believe it if I hadn't seen it with my own eyes. You certainly seem to have discovered a wonderful new way with people over the summer," Barbie said brightly. But was that a hint of suspicion Dawn could hear under her sweet words?

"Maybe eighth grade just brings out the friendliness in people," Dawn said airily. She made an effort to match Barbie's ultra-shiny smile with one of her own.

"Maybe," Barbie said. "Anyway, I think all the attention you seem to be getting is great. Just great. What's your secret?"

"Secret?" Dawn repeated. "Um, nothing. No secret." She crossed her fingers behind her back. *No secret except syzygy,* she added to herself. *But that's for me to know and you not to find out.* Having magical powers was the best. But that could change if Barbie ever discovered the truth.

"Hey, big sister! Glad I caught you."

Wonder of wonders! Even Paul wanted to talk to Dawn this afternoon. In fact he was waiting in front of her Social Studies class before the bell.

"Jen told me I could find you here. I forgot to say thanks for doing D-day today." D-day meant dinner duty—chopping vegetables, scrubbing pots, drying dishes, and whatever other horrible chores their mom could think up.

"You came by to say thank you?" Dawn wished she had a tape recorder. This was a moment worth saving.

"Yeah. Is it a crime to thank someone for doing you a favor?" Paul sounded embarrassed at his own politeness.

Dawn giggled. "No, it's very sweet of you. I'm just not used to having a sweet little brother." She couldn't resist some teasing. It occurred to Dawn that once Paul turned thirteen, he would be doing some magical teasing of his own. But right now, she was the one in control.

Paul looked as if he wanted to come back with a really good retort. But something was stopping him. Well, not just any old something. The popularity spell. He couldn't hang on to his smart-aleck grin, despite years of practice. "Well, it was sweet of *you* to help me out," Paul wound up saying. "These junior varsity try outs are really big news."

"No problem, Paul. Once you get picked for the basketball team, you can take my turn at D-day as often as you want," Dawn kidded.

"How exciting!" Paul said. In a more serious tone, he added, "Hey, do you really think I'll make the team?"

"Definitely. At least one of us ought to be happy about being such a beanpole." The second bell echoed in the hall. "Well, listen, good luck at the try outs, okay?"

"Yeah. Hey, and thanks again."

"Sure thing," Dawn said sincerely. Paul could be a pest sometimes, but he could also be a pretty good kid. Especially when he said thank you twice in the space of about two minutes. Popularity certainly had its advantages.

"Well, Dawn Powell. Hello, dear. How was your summer?" Mrs. Kronovitch leaned across her desk. "Nice to have you back in my class."

Mrs. Kronovitch smiling at her? And asking about her summer? It wasn't just the kids who were under this spell. It was the teachers, too! "Uh, my summer was very good, Mrs. Kronovitch," Dawn said, taking out her Social Studies book. "And yours?"

"Quite pleasant. And aren't you a gem for asking?" Mrs. Kronovitch remarked.

Megan leaned across the aisle and jabbed Dawn with her index finger. "I don't believe it," she whispered out of the side of her mouth. "You told me she was never nice to anyone."

It was true. And until right now, Dawn had dreaded having Mrs. Kronovitch two years in a row. But with a little magic, the old sourpuss had sweetened up. Dawn flipped her loose-leaf open to the section labeled "Social Studies." A ripple of worry ran through her. Would she be known as a teacher's pet, the way Mary Beth Carter was? Would people whisper "goody-goody" as she walked by?

"I'm impressed," Megan whispered. "If Mrs. Renzulli likes you half as much, I'd say we've got a pretty good chance at getting that duet in choir."

Would it be that easy? Dawn wondered. With the popularity spell, maybe she wouldn't have to be the best singer, only the one Mrs. Renzulli liked best. Come to think of it, her spell probably explained why Megan and the other kids couldn't possibly consider her a teacher's pet. Dawn Powell, formerly a shy, quiet wallflower was now the most popular person at Crestfield Middle School—with the students *and* the teachers. Dawn grinned at the thought.

Mrs. Kronovitch rapped her pointer on the chalkboard, her signal that class was about to begin. Dawn took out a pen and wrote the date on top of a clean sheet of loose-leaf paper. She tried to turn her attention to her first Social Studies class of the year, but it was hard to concentrate. She kept thinking about her spell. It was great to be the undisputed star of school for a day. But had she gotten there fairly? It was just too easy. She hadn't even worked at it.

Dawn doodled a big, curly question mark in the margin of her notebook. Maybe this afternoon, when she told Jennifer her big secret, her cousin would have some advice. Next to the question mark in her notebook margin, Dawn drew a bold exclamation point.

Dawn looked up at the usually sour Social Studies teacher. Her helmet of black hair bobbed up and down as she covered the chalkboard with a list of names and dates. When she turned back around, Dawn returned her smile. Maybe Mrs. Kronovitch wasn't half bad after all.

Six

When the final bell rang, Dawn raced down the hall. She could see the back of Jennifer's red shirt as her cousin headed out the door. She rushed to catch up with her.

But before she got very far, her path was blocked by Cindy Mitchell. "Dawn!" She put a hand on Dawn's arm. "I just wanted to tell you how glad I am that you're coming this weekend."

The popularity spell strikes again, Dawn thought. She looked down the hall and saw Jennifer leaving the building. What bad timing! Still, it was kind of nice that Cindy had finally discovered Dawn Powell was alive.

"I'm glad I'm coming, too, Cindy," Dawn said. "But listen, if you don't mind, I have to try and catch up with Jennifer. I'll see you tomorrow, okay?"

"Sure. Sue and I will save a seat for you at lunch."

"Great. Bye." Dawn sprinted toward the exit. Oh, no! Out of the corner of her eye she saw Gary Elwood hurrying toward her. She knew his schoolbag was filled with math texts. And somewhere in there was the new equation that he desperately wanted to share with her.

"Gary, forgive me for this," Dawn whispered under her breath.

> *Your feet will not move.*
> *They'll stay glued to the floor*
> *Until I have passed*
> *And have gone out the door.*

Dawn arched her eyebrow. Gary stopped in his tracks. Dawn could see him straining to pull his feet free of the gray linoleum, but they wouldn't come loose. A wave of shame washed over her. This was not the right way to use such special powers. But if she got stuck looking at Gary's equation, she'd never catch up to Jennifer.

She walked swiftly to the school doors. The sooner she left the building, the sooner poor Gary could pry his shoes off the floor. And the sooner she could finally tell Jennifer about her huge secret. Dawn's stomach filled with butterflies. Jennifer *had* to be excited about her magical powers. If not, well, Dawn knew they wouldn't seem half as exciting to her anymore.

She pulled open the heavy doors and blinked in the bright afternoon sunlight. She didn't see her cousin anywhere. But there were plenty of other kids around. Donna Lee gave her a big wave. Joanie Davis called out Dawn's name. A boy Dawn recognized from French class came over to tell her what a good accent she had. A girl Dawn had never seen before complimented her on the ribbon in her hair.

For the umpteenth time that day, Dawn felt a thrill at being a middle school celebrity. Her! Shy, quiet Dawn Powell. But she also saw her chance to talk to Jennifer slipping away. If she let Jennifer out of her sight, Dawn wouldn't have a chance to catch up with her. And then she'd have to go straight home to help her mother in the kitchen.

For a minute, Dawn considered putting the holding spell she'd used on Gary on all the kids around her now. But then she wondered if her magic was strong enough for such a big undertaking. And besides, how many times in your life did you get to be the most popular girl in your whole school?

Dawn decided to enjoy the attention. She could always tell Jennifer another time.

"Dawn, sweetheart, what did you do? Put a spell on those kids?"

Dawn helped herself to some mashed potatoes. "Well, Dad, what would you say if I told you I had?" She flashed a joking smile. *If they only knew!*

Her mother laughed. "I'd say I believed you. I haven't heard the phone ring so much since April and her friends were trying to decide what to wear to the prom last year." She speared a brussels sprout with her fork.

"Mom!" April protested. "Maybe instead of making fun of me, you could listen to what I'm trying to tell you about this new exchange student." She sounded frustrated. "It's bad enough that the phone keeps ringing every two seconds."

"You're just jealous," Paul said. Now that he was under the same spell as the rest of the middle school, he was Dawn's biggest defender. "For once, the phone calls are for someone besides you."

"Paul . . ." Mrs. Powell scolded, drawing her dark eyebrows together. "We're all happy that eighth grade seems to agree with Dawn, but that's no reason to be rude to April."

When neither parent was looking, April stuck out her tongue at Paul. Then she smiled at her mother like an angel. With her blond curls and round, pink cheeks, she could fit the part when she wanted to. "So, about this exchange student," she said eagerly. "He's from Europe. Spain, I think."

He. *Well, that figures,* Dawn thought. *No wonder April wants to discuss the new member of her class.*

"He's really cute. And he has this adorable accent and—"

BRRING!

"Oh, for heaven's sake!" April exclaimed. But it didn't stop her from jumping up from the table. "Maybe this time it's for *me,*" she said. But in a few

71

seconds she was back. "Guess who it's for?" She plunked herself back down and stabbed at her chicken.

"For me?" Dawn went into the kitchen and picked up the receiver. "Hello?"

"Hi. Boy, who's been on the phone all night?" Megan's voice came over the line.

"Megan! Hi!" Dawn was happy it wasn't another magically charmed admirer calling. Not that she didn't like all her new friends. But there was something nice about knowing that Megan would have called anyway, magic or not. "Well, you know how the first day of school is," Dawn said. "Lots of people have been calling to talk about it." She managed to avoid adding that all the calls had been for her. Megan must think she was a real social butterfly at school. But it wasn't really true. At least not under *normal* circumstances.

"So, have you worked on our song for the audition yet?" Megan asked.

Dawn got an uncomfortable feeling in her stomach. And it wasn't because she'd been wolfing down dinner between phone calls. "No, not yet. It's been kind of nuts around here."

"Oh." Megan's voice was small.

"But don't worry. I will," Dawn said quickly.

"Okay." There was a pause that seemed to last an eternity. "This is really important to me."

"Me, too. I'll definitely be ready to practice the song with you at lunch tomorrow."

"Great." Megan sounded happier. "See you then."

"Bye, Megan." Dawn hung up the receiver. She felt a cold slap of reality. Not only hadn't she practiced the choir piece, she also hadn't practiced for her guitar lesson yet, or gotten to any of her homework. And there wasn't going to be time for her usual first day of school gab with Jennifer. Or time to share the biggest secret of her whole life with her cousin.

Being popular was fun, alright, but it definitely took up a lot of time.

"Let's just take the receiver off the hook," April suggested as Dawn sat back down at the table. "It doesn't look like I'm going to get any calls, anyway." She sounded a little sorry for herself.

Actually, Dawn thought, *that isn't a bad idea.* It would give her a chance to do her homework and practice her song.

But Dawn's father shook his head. "Can't,

honey. Mom and I are working on getting Tim Timber to do a special video with us. We have to be available for his agent's call."

"Tim Timber, the country singer?" April put her fork down. Her eyes opened wide.

"None other," Mrs. Powell said. "If we can get him for our next project, I think it would really give our new company a push in the right direction."

"Wow!" April's eyes glazed over. "Tim Timber, right here in Crestfield. Working with *my* parents." Dawn could understand how her sister felt—and she wasn't even as big a country music fan as April was.

"Maybe," Mr. Powell reminded her. "We haven't heard anything definite yet."

April seemed to think about that. "Oh. Well, then, I guess I'd better calm down," she said.

Dawn felt a tug of surprise. Since when had April gotten so practical.

"I've got my exchange student to think about, anyway." A silly grin appeared on April's face.

Dawn made a face and rolled her eyes. This exchange student must really be special to distract her sister from one of her favorite stars.

"The problem is that half the girls in my class are just dying for Pablo to ask them out," April added with a sigh. "I don't know if I have a chance."

Maybe I should have put the popularity spell on April, Dawn thought.

BRRING! The sound of the telephone interrupted dinner again. Four faces immediately turned to Dawn. She threw her hands up in the air. "Okay, okay. I'll get it!" She pushed herself away from the table and ran happily to the phone. Eighth grade was going to be a magical year. Dawn just wondered when she would ever be able to get anything done.

"Find the value of x when x is twice y and y equals eight," Dawn read. Sometimes it helped to say the equations out loud. But tonight, nothing seemed to help. She was so tired her eyelids kept closing.

Upstairs the rest of her family had been asleep for hours. Dawn had waited until they all went to bed. Then she had sneaked down to the living room with a pile of unfinished homework. At least she'd managed to practice her audition piece for a while, but there was still more schoolwork to do. If only she hadn't spent so much of the evening on the phone.

Now the numbers swam in front of her eyes. Where was Gary Elwood when she needed him? A picture of Gary flashed through Dawn's mind. She could remember exactly how he had looked in the hall at school, straining to move his feet, a look of bewilderment on his face. Dawn felt a stab of remorse over casting the spell. It had made her feel mean, and it wasn't like her to be mean. But then, it wasn't like Dawn to be so popular, either.

Today had been one of the most fun first days of school ever. But now Dawn was starting to wonder if she had had enough of being popular. On one hand, it would be comforting to go back to being herself—her medium-popular self, with time for her guitar and her schoolwork and the friends that mattered most. On the other hand, there was her reserved seat at the "in" table, Danny Page's attention, Mrs. Kronovitch's smile, and all the other benefits of being popular. Dawn wasn't sure what she wanted.

She yawned. One thing was certain, though. She still had a page of math problems to finish. She stared at the equations in her notebook. At the rate she was going, she'd be stuck on "y equals eight" until some time next year. Maybe it had been too ambitious to take Accelerated Math. Dawn felt as if she'd have to be some kind of Albert Einstein to ever understand algebra.

Then inspiration struck. What if she had the math know-how of a person like Einstein just long enough to finish up her homework? Dawn felt certain it would be okay to use a little magic in the name of education. She remembered a picture she had once seen of the famous man. His white hair stuck out in all directions, and he looked like a movie version of a mad scientist. But there wasn't a chance he'd be stuck on the value of x for very long. Dawn chanted softly:

> *Math problems large,*
> *And math problems small,*
> *Are no problem for me,*
> *I know them all.*

She arched her eyebrow. And waited. Somehow, she had expected the solution to her homework problem to ring out in her head. But when she looked down at the equation, she wasn't any more certain about x than she'd been before. Had she made some mistake when she'd cast her spell? She thought about the day she'd conjured up the cheese-flavored milk. Were her powers giving out on her again?

"Are you the young lady who brought me here?" Dawn whirled around as she heard a voice behind her.

Dawn gasped. A small man with a droopy mustache and a heavily lined face was sitting in the middle of her living room. "Are you . . . Albert Einstein?"

"You did call me, didn't you?" he asked.

"Well—not exactly," Dawn stammered. What had she done wrong? Maybe she'd been picturing Mr. Einstein a little too hard when she'd cast her spell. "I mean, not that you're not welcome!" She stumbled over her words. What was she supposed to say to a legend like Albert Einstein?

Mr. Einstein turned around slowly. He seemed to be studying the glass table on its metal frame, the couch, the TV with the V.C.R. "Late twentieth century, I'd guess. A little after my time, certainly."

Dawn nodded. "Won't you have a seat?" she managed to say, motioning to the old armchair.

Such an important guest should definitely have the most comfortable seat in the house.

Mr. Einstein settled into the armchair. "Very cozy. I'd forgotten some of the pleasures of this little piece of the universe. So," he said, "I suppose you're one of those people who can harness some of those powers I never learned about during my stay in the world." He shook his head, and his shaggy hair danced around his face. "There's so much I didn't discover until much later. But enough about me, Miss—"

"Dawn," Dawn said. She couldn't believe she had forgotten to introduce herself. Even if Albert Einstein was sitting in her living room and she was in shock, she still should have remembered her manners.

Mr. Einstein cocked one bushy, white eyebrow. "So, Dawn, if you didn't call me here on purpose, how did I happen to get here?"

Dawn could feel herself blushing. "Well, I'm sort of new at this, and well, I wasn't actually trying to bring you here. I only wanted to know what you know for a few minutes."

"Well, if you want my mind, I guess you have to take all of me." Mr. Einstein's eyes crinkled with amusement. "Now what did you need to know so very badly that you thought my knowledge could help you out?"

"It's my math homework," Dawn explained. Saying it out loud, she realized that it was silly to expect such a great man to help her with a few xs and ys.

Mr. Einstein smiled. "Math homework, eh? What's the problem?" He fumbled in the breast pocket of his rumpled jacket, and pulled out a pair of wire-rimmed spectacles.

Dawn stretched out her arm to hand Mr. Einstein her math book. But she froze as she heard footsteps on the stairs.

"Dawn?" Her mother's voice drifted into the living room. "Dawn, wake up!"

Dawn felt someone shaking her shoulders. What was happening? She opened one eye. Her mother was standing over her, and Mr. Einstein was nowhere in sight. Sun flooded the living room through the open curtains. Dawn slammed her eye shut against the bright light. She felt around with one hand, trying to make some sense of her surroundings. She was lying on the living room couch. It was morning. And that meant her visit from Albert Einstein had been nothing more than a dream.

"Dawn! Come on, honey, you're late. You overslept."

Dawn opened her eyes again. "Mom?" Her voice came out croaky.

"What are you doing down here, Dawn?"

Dawn pushed herself up on one elbow. Her body felt sore and cramped. She had fallen asleep with her legs tucked under her. Her schoolbooks had slipped to the floor.

"I guess you wouldn't believe me if I said I'd come down for a late night snack," Dawn said lamely. She felt a little sad that she'd only dreamed Mr. Einstein. He seemed like such a nice man. Not to mention that he'd been about to help her with the homework that lay unfinished on the carpet.

"You came down for a snack with all your schoolbooks? Honey, I'm happy that it's important to you to get your homework finished. But the time to do it was yesterday evening instead of talking on the phone." Her mother was stern. "I really don't understand this. It's so unlike you to put your social life before your schoolwork. I hope this isn't going to be a new pattern this year."

"I'm sorry, Mom." Dawn got up and stretched her legs. She was still in yesterday's jeans and boating shirt.

"Well, we can talk about it later," her mother said. "You're very late. Paul left early for a trial scrimmage and April's just about to leave. I suggest you wash up and grab a muffin on your way out. I'll call Uncle Kenneth's and tell Jennifer not to wait for you."

"Oh, no, Mom! I'll be ready in a second!" Dawn had missed her chance to swap first day of school stories with Jennifer yesterday. She wanted to do some catching up on the way to school today. And, more important, she wanted to finally let Jennifer in on her birthday discovery. "I can catch Jennifer if I hurry!"

"Dawn, it's not fair to make your cousin late, too. If you wanted to walk to school with her, you should have thought about it when you were talking to all your friends."

Dawn sighed and went up to her room to change. According to her alarm clock, she had to be at school in ten minutes. Which was about how long it took to get there. She started moving more quickly. She hurriedly shed her creased, slept-in clothes. Not only was she going to show up on the second day of school without her homework, but she was going to be late, too.

She splashed her face with warm water and pulled a brush through her hair. Her stomach hurt. She wasn't used to being in trouble in school. She had never been in a situation like this before the magic had come along.

She pulled on her denim skirt and a clean T-shirt. She shoved her feet into her sandals and threw her schoolbooks into her knapsack. Slinging the bag over one shoulder, she raced downstairs. She could get to school faster if she took her new bike, but it sure would be easier if she could pop into school by—

—by magic! Was it possible that she could move herself from home to school just the way she'd moved the Frisbee on her birthday? She took a bran muffin from the kitchen and yelled good-bye to her parents. As soon as she was out the door and out of view, she concentrated on a mental image of the school. Then she arched her eyebrow.

The ground seemed to melt beneath her feet. The familiar sights of Caroline Street wavered and blurred. Her body felt warm and limp, as if she were sinking into a hot bath. The stately oak tree in the Pages' front yard grew fuzzy and transparent. Dawn could see the blue sky behind it. Then it disappeared altogether as her feet lost contact with the ground.

Seven

Dawn was terrified. The world she knew had disappeared in an instant. Her arms flailed wildly in space. Lights and colors whirled around her, like a kaleidoscope gone crazy.

But her fear gave way to the warm, tingly feeling in her body, and the breathtaking spiral rainbow spinning around her. She floated weightlessly through the sea of colors. Then, all too quickly, the outline of Crestfield Middle School began materializing behind the pieces of this strange, multicolored world. Dawn could see kids streaming into the school entrance. Her feet touched ground. The funny feeling in her body stopped. She had arrived at school just a split second after walking out her door.

"Dawn! Heavens! How did you sneak up so suddenly!"

Dawn whirled around. Barbie Davison. Of course. That girl always seemed to be around at the worst times.

"I could have sworn you weren't here a second ago," Barbie said. "Even though I'm happy to see you," she added—thanks to the popularity spell, Dawn was sure.

Dawn hoped her laugh didn't sound too forced. "Trick photography?" she suggested.

"Trick something," Barbie answered.

"Maybe your eyes are playing tricks on you," Dawn suggested. She put on a concerned face. "You know, Barbie, between what happened in Ms. Davenport's class yesterday, and this, well, I'm a little worried about you." Actually, Dawn didn't have to try too hard to look concerned. She was— concerned that Barbie had seen a little too much.

"Well, well." Jennifer came up behind Dawn.

"Jen!" Even though Dawn had seen her cousin just the day before, it seemed much longer ago. Probably because she felt as if she and Jennifer had so much catching up to do. "Hi! I'm really sorry I couldn't walk with you this morning."

"Yeah, I know. You were late," Jennifer said. "So late that you managed to get here before me. Barbie, will you excuse us? I need to talk to my cousin in private."

Oops. Dawn hadn't thought about this complication. "Jen, I *was* late for school," she insisted as they walked away from Barbie. "I just, well—" Well, what? How was she going to explain this?

"Oh, I understand," Jennifer said.

"You do?"

"Sure. You were too busy with all your new friends." Dawn heard the hurt in Jennifer's voice. "The ones you were on the phone with all last night."

Dawn stopped walking. "How'd you know?"

"Every time I tried to call you, your line was busy. So I figured I'd let you call me."

"I wanted to, but . . ."

"But what?" Jennifer tossed her blond curls. "Honestly, Dawn. I know we talked about you being a little more outgoing this year, and I'm really happy you're making new friends, but don't you think you can still spare a little time for me?"

Dawn noticed that Jennifer had her flower pin tacked to her shirt, the one that squirted water at people who got close enough. But Jennifer was clearly not in the mood for practical jokes right now.

So much for being protected by the popularity spell. Perhaps when feelings were strong enough, not even magic could change them. Dawn realized that Jennifer would probably have been three times more upset without the spell. But it wasn't much consolation.

"Jen, it's not what you think," Dawn said. They headed toward the school's front door. "I'm not purposely trying to be the center of attention. And I really did leave the house a second ago."

Jennifer's blue eyes flashed. "Boy, first you stand me up on the way to school. Then you make up some unbelievable story to get out of it." Jennifer's hurt turned to anger. "I don't get it, Dawn. Ever since school started you've been like another person."

Dawn felt a wave of unhappiness wash over her. Maybe it was true. Would the old Dawn have talked on the phone all night and left her homework undone? Would the old Dawn have hidden her biggest discovery from her best friend?

No. And Dawn was starting to realize that she liked it better the old way. She took a huge breath, crossed her fingers behind her back for good luck, and took the dive.

"Listen, Jen. I know you think something's going on. And you're right." As she began, Dawn could feel her heart pumping as if she'd run all the way to school on her own two feet. "For starters, I wasn't making it up when I said I just left for school a second ago."

Jennifer put on a fake smile and cocked her head. "I get it. You just flew over here, right?"

"Well, sort of. Not in an airplane or anything. But . . . Jen, do you remember the magic game we used to play when we were little?"

"When we pretended we could zap things from one place to another and make people do stuff," Jennifer said. "Are you telling me you were late because you were playing some dumb game we made up ages ago?"

Dawn looked to her right. Then to her left. Most of the kids were already inside, but a few latecomers straggled toward the door. As Dawn turned to look behind her, Sue Flagg waved madly. Dawn gave a distracted wave back. Then she leaned over and whispered in Jennifer's ear. "Jen, that magic game isn't so dumb. And it isn't pretend anymore. Not for me."

Jennifer gave a short laugh. "Boy, and you're always telling me *I'm* the one with the imagination. Why don't you quit while you're only a little behind? Next you're going to try to convince me that you saw a ghost or something."

Dawn felt herself stiffen. "I didn't see one. I am one. I mean, not a ghost. A *something*." There. She'd said it. She held her breath and waited for Jennifer's reaction.

"I think your ribbon's tied too tight," Jennifer pushed open the school's door.

As she followed her cousin, Dawn felt a bubble of despair rising inside her. She had tried to tell Jennifer the biggest secret in the whole world, and Jennifer didn't believe a word of it.

"Hey, Dawn!" called Liza Martin.

"Hi, Liza."

"How're you doing?" a boy in Dawn's Math class asked as he passed by.

"Okay," Dawn answered, forcing a smile. If only she could give Jennifer a demonstration. But with all these people around, she didn't dare.

"Listen, Dawn, I'll give you points for creativity," Jennifer said. "But that's about it." She shook her head. "I'd think seriously about squirting you with my flower, but I don't want to waste the water." She gave a sniff and turned on the heel of her hightops.

Dawn watched Jennifer's back as she disappeared into the crowd of students. A lump formed in her throat. She felt miserable. Miserable and alone. Even though the second Jennifer left, Dawn was surrounded by classmates under the influence of the popularity spell.

The instant attention only made Dawn more aware of what she was missing—real friendship, the kind that came from honest feelings. The kind she had with Jennifer when she wasn't busy being the most popular person in school. There was only one thing to do.

I wish I wasn't at all popular, Dawn thought to herself. Good-bye Miss Crestfield Middle School. Good-bye popularity spell. She arched her eyebrow.

And then a funny thing happened. The sea of people around her seemed to part. Kids who had been jostling each other to get her attention now moved away from her. Almost before Dawn knew what was happening, she was standing by herself.

"Whoa! I didn't mean to scare people off that badly," she mumbled. But she really did feel relieved. She could breathe again. She was herself.

She headed for homeroom, past Cindy Mitchell's locker. "Hi, Cindy," she said.

Cindy looked Dawn right in the eye. Then she wrinkled up her nose and quickly turned away. Dawn stared after her, confused. Now that she wasn't the most popular, she didn't expect to be the first one on Cindy and Sue's top ten list. But Cindy had never been so mean before.

Dawn tried to shrug it off. Maybe it was better than having Cindy brimming with friendliness she didn't usually feel. Dawn had done without her attention before. She could do without it again. Even if it hurt.

As Dawn rounded the corner, she caught sight of a mop of red curls at the end of the hallway. "Megan!" she called. "Megan, hi!" She waved her arm over her head and rushed toward her friend. "Hey, I worked on the piece," she announced.

"Oh," Megan said flatly. Was she still angry from last night? She had seemed okay when they had gotten off the phone. Maybe she just needed a little coaxing.

"It's really pretty. And the soprano part isn't that hard," Dawn said brightly.

Megan didn't even respond. She just turned to go and said, "Listen, Dawn, I don't want to be late for class." It seemed as if she couldn't wait to get away.

"Megan, what's wrong?" Dawn was getting a cold feeling in her fingers and toes.

"Nothing," Megan said. But her tone of voice gave her away. What was happening? It was as if Dawn had done *too* good a job of taking back her spell. She searched her mind for the exact words she had been thinking when she'd lifted the popularity spell. *I wish I wasn't at all* . . . yes, that was it. *I wish I wasn't at all popular.*

Oh, no! Dawn hadn't said she wished she was back to normal. She hadn't said she wanted to take back her spell. She had been in such a hurry that she hadn't even bothered to compose a careful poem.

No, she had only wished she wasn't *at all* popular. As in not the slightest bit. As in totally, completely unpopular. The reality hit her like a failing grade on an exam. Dawn Powell, recently the best-liked girl at Crestfield Middle School, was now a complete outcast.

Eight

"Dawn Powell!" Mrs. Kronovitch's sharp, shrill voice echoed off the walls.

Dawn whipped around. Her Social Studies teacher wore a nasty expression as she peered out of her classroom door.

"Young lady, are you practicing to be a lawn decoration?"

"Excuse me?" Dawn didn't know quite what Mrs. Kronovitch meant. But she was certain it wasn't anything good. Good-bye to being on the receiving end of one of the cranky teacher's rare smiles.

"A lawn decoration," Mrs. Kronovitch repeated.

"A statue. Standing in one place like that. Didn't you hear the second bell ring?" Clearly, Dawn was as unpopular with Mrs. Kronovitch as she was with everyone else around here.

Dawn shrugged nervously. What could she say? That she was in the middle of composing a spell to take back a spell to take back a spell?

"I'd suggest you get to homeroom right this instant, or I'll have to report you to Mr. Hawkins."

Dawn groaned. The last thing she needed on what had already become the worst day of her life was to be sent to the Hawk! She'd better start moving. But before she went to class as the most disliked girl at Crestfield Middle School, she needed to undo the spell.

Twice Dawn had arched her eyebrow thoughtlessly. And twice she had wound up with a spell she hadn't intended to cast. She couldn't mess up this time. Her thoughts had to be carefully focused and precisely worded if she wanted to get out of this jam. Dawn looked over at Mrs. Kronovitch's sour expression. This situation was getting more complicated by the minute.

"I don't intend to stand here and face off, either," Mrs. Kronovitch said curtly.

Well, thank you very much for the suggestion, Mrs. Kronovitch, Dawn thought. She raised her eyebrow. That should hold the impatient teacher long enough for Dawn to do what she had to do.

But Mrs. Kronovitch was still in gear. "I said now!" she hollered.

What was going on? Mrs. Kronovitch was supposed to be out of commission. Dawn arched her eyebrow again. "Hold her there for a minute or two. Hold her there until I'm through," she whispered to herself.

"If you have something to say, I'd advise you to say it to my face," Mrs. Kronovitch said. Dawn arched her eyebrow desperately. "I'm not playing games," the Social Studies teacher added.

Dawn's stomach did a queasy somersault. Her powers had given out. Right here. At the worst possible time. She *had* been using an awful lot of magic in the past two days: The popularity spell. The spell on Barbie. The one on Gary. Then there was the spell to get to school, and, most unfortunately, the spell that had made her totally unpopular.

She should have realized that it was only a matter of time before her powers reached their limit. Now she had no idea how long she's have to wait before her magic batteries got recharged. All she knew was that Jennifer wasn't feeling overly friendly. Nor was Megan. Not Mrs. Kronovitch. Nor anyone else in the entire school. When she reversed the popularity spell she had traded Tollhouse cookies for cold stares, and right now there wasn't a single thing she could do about it. Dawn blinked back a tear, hiked up her knapsack, and headed for class.

After an awful morning, it was finally time for lunch, an hour Dawn had especially been dreading. She forked up a soggy french fry. This was exactly what she had been afraid of—sitting by herself in the middle of a crowded lunchroom. She had a whole table to herself. *If it weren't raining, everyone would probably be scrambling to take their lunch outside,* Dawn thought. *As far away from me as possible.*

She forced herself to take a bite of her hamburger. The meat had no flavor and the roll tasted like cardboard. She put it down and pushed her tray away. She didn't have much of an appetite.

Across the lunchroom, Jennifer and Megan were sitting together. Dawn noticed that they were looking awfully chummy. Jennifer said something and Megan burst out laughing.

"Dawn?" Dawn looked up to find Cindy Mitchell standing over her. Dawn wasn't sure she had heard right. Was Cindy actually talking to her?

"Hi," Dawn said timidly, as if Cindy were a deer she didn't want to frighten away. Actually, after the way Cindy had behaved in the hall this morning, a poisonous snake was more like it. But Dawn was feeling pretty lonely. Even the company of Cindy was better than feeling like the invisible girl. "Wanna sit down?"

Cindy made a face as if she had eaten something bad. "Oh, no. I couldn't possibly. I just came by to tell you that—well—my mother says I invited too many people to the slumber party. So I—"

"I understand," Dawn said quickly. She could feel her face growing hot with embarrassment. She blinked rapidly against the salty sting of tears.

"Good," Cindy said. "I knew you'd take it okay." Without a second glance, she hurried away.

She couldn't have run off any faster if she were trying out for the track team, Dawn thought miserably. One tear got away, and she wiped her cheek with her sleeve. But another tear immediately followed. Dawn couldn't hold them back any longer. Big, fat tears rolled down her cheeks. Her body shook. She didn't think it could get any worse.

But she was wrong. Jennifer and Megan picked that second, the worst possible second, to walk by with their trays. Through the blur of tears, Dawn saw them looking at her. She fought to get control of herself. She couldn't let the entire school see her blubbering in the middle of the lunchroom like a baby. But she couldn't stop crying. Dawn put her head in her hands.

"Hey! Come on, Dawn!"

Jennifer? Dawn picked her head up. Her sobs quieted. Jennifer slid in next to her on the bench. Dawn held her breath. Was this going to be a variation of the Cindy Mitchell story? Was Jennifer here to remind her just how unwanted she was around school? This morning Jennifer's anger had been strong enough to overcome even the popularity spell itself. Maybe that would happen again, in reverse.

"You know I'm mad at you," Jennifer began. Dawn's heart sank into her stomach. "But I hate to see you like this," she continued. A note of compassion found its way into her voice.

For the first time that day, Dawn gave in to a tiny smile. "Don't think this means we're making up or anything," Jennifer was quick to add. Dawn felt the smile slipping away.

"It's just that, well, I don't know," Jennifer fumbled. "One part of me doesn't want to have anything to do with you. And believe me, I've got plenty of company. You know, Megan's thinking of finding someone else to audition with."

Just as Dawn was on the verge of tears again, Jennifer did another abrupt about-face. "Listen, I'm not telling you this to get you all upset. I'm just trying to say in spite of it, I can't stand for you to be sitting here crying. I mean, one part of me can't. And one part of me . . . well, it's hard to explain." Jennifer struggled with the emotions that were pulling her in different directions.

But Dawn didn't have a bit of trouble understanding. The backfired spell made Jennifer feel one way. The friendship the two of them shared made her feel just the opposite. The problem was trying to explain it.

"Listen, Jen. It's like I was telling you this morning," Dawn began. "You're under a magic spell. That's why you can't decide how you're feeling."

Jennifer groaned. "Oh, not this again."

"Jennifer, you've got to listen to me. I'm not making this up. I swear."

Jennifer's frown deepened. "I almost think you believe what you're saying."

"Jen, I do."

"Show me!" Jennifer challenged.

Dawn slumped down on the cafeteria bench. For starters, she couldn't put on a magic show with all these people around. Now that she was so unpopular, they'd think she was doubly weird if they found out about her. But even if she had dared, what could she do with her powers all run down? Nothing, that was what.

Jennifer drummed her fingers impatiently on the table. "I knew it!" she said. "I come over to try to make you feel better, and all you want to do is make up a huge excuse again." She got up. "I know something's going on with you. It's almost as if they took the real Dawn away and replaced her with someone who just looks like Dawn. When you're ready to tell me the truth, I'm ready to listen."

The truth! Dawn had tried. And failed. The truth was that Dawn was almost beginning to be sorry she had ever discovered her powers in the first place.

"I don't deserve to have powers!" Back at home that afternoon, Dawn poured her heart out to the only person who could possibly understand. "Grandma, I've made such a mess."

"Fiddlesticks!" Her grandmother's creaky voice came over the phone line. "Everyone who's just starting out makes some mistakes. It's only natural. And it's the only way to learn."

"But, Grandma, you warned me. You told me not to depend on my powers too much, and I didn't listen. If this were a class, I'd get an F." Dawn sat cross-legged, cradling the phone in her lap.

Grandma Cassie laughed. "When have you ever gotten an F in anything, my dear?"

"Never. I mean, until now."

"Come, come. It won't help to feel sorry for yourself, you know. That never got anyone out of a bind."

"I don't feel sorry for myself. I'm angry. How could I be so dumb?"

"Dumb? I don't think so," her grandmother assured her. "In fact, I'd wager that you know more now than you did before all this happened."

Dawn considered this for a moment. "I suppose so," she finally agreed. "I know that it's better to be myself, even if I'm not the most popular girl in school."

"That sounds like a big lesson to me," Grandma Cassie said approvingly. "Do you know the expression 'to thine own self be true'?"

"I guess I should keep it in mind, huh?" Dawn asked.

"I guess so."

"But I've still got a big problem. Everyone in school hates me. And Jennifer doesn't believe that I'm magic. And without my powers, I can't do a thing about it."

"Well, dear, I'm not going to be much help where your powers are concerned. You're simply going to have to be patient and wait for them to come back. And as for Jennifer, well, we all need one special person to confide in. If Jennifer is that person, you'll simply have to give her a little magic show whenever you're able."

"And until then, I guess I'll have to go on being the least-liked person at school." Dawn said.

"Well, I do believe your old grandmother may just have a few tricks up her sleeve for neutralizing bad spells."

"You do?" Dawn wished Grandma Cassie was right there, so she could give her a huge kiss.

"Of course, I might have more success if I didn't have to do this over the phone. Dawn, how would you like to take a little trip to visit me?"

"Grandma, I'd love to, but how am I supposed to get there? Mom and Dad aren't around to drive me. Besides, they've been working really hard on some big video they think Tim Timber is going to do with them."

"Tim Timber, the country singer?" Dawn couldn't believe it. Her grandma sounded almost as gushy as April. "Oh, if only I were forty years younger," she said.

"Grandma!"

"Oh, you'll discover boys one day, too, my dear. But never mind that for now. I wasn't thinking of having you come up by car. Are you ready to go now?"

"I guess."

"All right, then, just relax. You're going to feel a bit peculiar for a few seconds, but don't be frightened. It's simply a minor rearrangement of space and matter."

"Huh?"

"It means I'm going to bring you here by a route most people never get to take," Grandma Cassie said.

"Oh, I see." Dawn figured out what her grandmother was getting at. "You're going to zap me over magically and you don't want me to be afraid of those weird flashing lights. Well, why didn't you just say so, Grandma?"

"Oh, you've traveled this way before?" She sounded surprised.

"To school," Dawn explained. "It's really fun."

"Hmm. You certainly have learned quite a lot in a few days," her grandmother mused. "Well, in that case, get ready."

Her voice faded and the telephone began to blur. The walls in the hallway grew fuzzy. Dawn had the same warm, weak feeling in her body that she had had on her magical trip to school that morning. But this time she was ready. She soaked up as much of the rainbow light show and tingly warmth as she could before her grandmother's round, smiling face materialized in the whirlwind of spinning shapes.

Dawn felt her feet make contact with firm ground. The swirling stopped. And there was Grandma Cassie, in an old pair of jeans and a sweatshirt. Her gray hair was pulled back with a colorful scarf. Her gardening gloves, still caked with dirt, lay by the telephone.

Dawn raced into her arms. Now she had the chance to kiss her grandmother in person. Grandma Cassie smelled of the herbs in her garden and that funny scented oil she wore instead of perfume.

"Let me get a look at you, my dear." She stepped back. Out the window behind her, Dawn could see Lake Michigan pounding against the shoreline. "My, my, how could anyone not like that face?" she said lightly.

"Grandma, this isn't funny," Dawn protested.

"Of course it isn't, dear," Grandma Cassie said quickly. "We'll take care of that nasty business right away. There will be time to chat afterwards. Oh, by the way, I wouldn't suggest trying a long trip like that on your own just yet. It takes some practice to be able to get this far. Stick to your own town for a while, all right?"

"From now on, I'm going to listen very carefully to everything you tell me," Dawn said. "That's another lesson I've learned." She followed Grandma Cassie across the pine floor to the tiny kitchen. Her grandmother boiled some water in an old copper tea kettle. Then she poured it into a cup and dropped in what looked like a bunch of twigs and leaves.

"What's that?" Dawn said nervously.

"Don't worry. It won't bite," Grandma Cassie said with a laugh. "It's not eye of newt or anything. Just raspberry tea. Cleans out the system. It helps when you're trying to get rid of a spell gone sour."

She put the tea on the kitchen table. She peered at it for a good minute or two. Dawn guessed that she was focusing her thoughts—the way Dawn tried to do when she made up a poem to go with her spell. Grandma Cassie's eyebrow shot up in an impressive arch. She took the tea and held it out. "To your health, my dear."

Dawn took the cup and sniffed. She took a tentative sip. It tasted surprisingly good. "Bottoms up," Grandma Cassie instructed. Dawn drank the warm tea as quickly as she could. "Good girl," her grand-mother said. "I now pronounce your social life back to normal."

"No sitting alone in the lunchroom?" Dawn asked. Her grandmother shook her head. "No more popularity princess either?"

"No more," Grandma Cassie confirmed.

"But no more powers for a while, either?" Dawn said, less happily.

"Oh, don't worry about that, dear. Your powers will come back. They always do."

"Even this time? Even if I haven't proved I'm ready to have them yet?"

"Nonsense." She sounded certain. "Your powers are part of you now, part of what make Dawn Powell a very special, magical thirteen-year-old."

Nine

"One petal from local flower in full bloom, one-quarter cup plain yogurt, one tablespoon wheat germ, half a banana, honey to taste . . ." A few days later, Dawn was finally getting around to copying down the magical health shake recipe her grandmother had given her. "Recite your name or name of person for whom shake is intended three times. Blend in blender or food processor," she wrote. Carefully, she transferred the rest of the recipe from the piece of note paper covered with her grandmother's slanted handwriting into her diary.

When she finished, she turned the piece of paper

over. *Love Potion,* Grandma Cassie had written on the other side. *Use with Caution.* Dawn skipped a line in her diary and began to write again. "Melt over double boiler, one small bag chocolate kisses. Add two teaspoons—"

"—Help!" April's scream shattered the afternoon. "Help! Fire! Someone hurry!" Dawn dropped her diary onto the bed and sprinted down the stairs. A cloud of smoke filled the kitchen. "April?" she yelled "Where are you?"

April's response was a fit of coughing. Dawn arched her eyebrow sharply. But instantly she realized that it wasn't going to do a bit of good. Her powers were still out. As she fought her way into the kitchen, she could see the source of the smoke: a charred frying pan on the stove. She groped her way to the sink, grabbed the spray attachment, and turned on the faucet full force. She aimed the spray right at the stove. But that only caused the pan to sizzle loudly.

"No!" April screamed. "You can't put water on a grease fire! Sand! We need sand!"

"Sand? In the middle of the kitchen? Get serious, April!"

"Good heavens!" Mrs. Powell's voice cut in from

the doorway. "What are you two girls doing?" She went to the cabinet under the sink and pulled out a bag of potting soil. Within seconds, the flames were smothered.

"Get some air in here!" she instructed. Dawn pulled the back door open, and smoke escaped onto the patio. As the haze cleared, Dawn saw that the stove was covered with soil. Good thing her mother had been too busy to get around to repotting the plants.

"April, " Mrs. Powell said wearily. "How did you manage to turn a few hamburgers into that smoky barbecue? I thought I asked you to keep on eye on them while they cooked."

"I was. I mean, I was just sitting here thinking and all of a sudden—" April waved her arms wildly.

"Thinking?" her mother echoed drily. "It must have been taking an awful lot of concentration for you not to have noticed that the burgers were burning."

April looked sheepish. "I guess I was thinking about Pablo again."

"Pablo?"

"The exchange student," Dawn explained. April had been going on about him the past two nights at bedtime, so Dawn knew exactly who her sister was talking about.

Mrs. Powell sighed. "That's all very well, dear, but next time you daydream, perhaps you could let us know so we can notify the fire department."

"Very funny, Mom," April said without cracking a smile.

Dawn thought about the love potion recipe she had been copying into her diary upstairs. Maybe that was the solution to April's problems. Dawn vowed to think any new magic spells through more carefully in the future than she had this week, but she'd have to give the love potion some serious consideration once her powers came back.

"What if I can't hit that high note?" Dawn took a final look at her music.

"Don't worry," Megan said. "When you're nervous, your voice gets higher." But Dawn could tell that Megan was just as scared as she was.

"Girls?" Mrs. Renzulli stuck her head out the classroom door. "I'm ready for you."

Dawn looked at Megan and crossed her fingers. "For luck," she whispered. Megan signaled back by showing her own crossed fingers.

Inside the choir room, Tad Johnstone and Donald McNeil were putting their music together and getting ready to leave. "Good luck," Tad said to Dawn and Megan. "Bye, Mrs. Renzulli."

"Good-bye, boys," Mrs. Renzulli answered. "You sounded very good. I can tell you practiced hard. Now, girls, don't look so frightened. Music should be a joyful experience." She smiled encouragingly and her round, soft face dimpled. *But even around someone as nice as Mrs. Renzulli,* thought Dawn, *it was still hard not to have a case of stage fright.*

The Music teacher propped her music sheet up on the piano. "It's a lovely little piece, isn't it?" She seated herself on the piano bench and played a few notes. "I love these old English folk songs."

Dawn nodded nervously. It was pretty. But what if she made some huge mistake? Or forgot her part? Megan was counting on her, too.

For a split second, Dawn wished she could give herself a little magic boost of confidence. But no. Even if her powers had been back, she knew it would be a bad thing. Winning the audition by magic wouldn't have been any more satisfying than being popular by magic.

115

"Ready when you are," Mrs. Renzulli said. Her fingers were poised over the keyboard.

Dawn took several very deep breaths. She looked at Megan. Megan nodded, and Mrs. Renzulli began playing the introduction. Megan's entrance was first. "Thy heart is sad," she sang in her warm voice.

"Thy smile rare," Dawn answered. Her first few notes were a little shaky.

"Let friendship heal thy every care," they sang together. As Dawn's higher notes blended with Megan's lower ones, her singing grew stronger and clearer.

Dawn closed her eyes and let the music surround her. She pretended she was onstage, performing to a rapt audience. The delicate tune swelled to fill the room. "Let friendship heal thy every care!" Dawn lingered on the last word and the high note sounded clear and true. Her voice rang out with Megan's. Then the room was quiet.

Dawn opened her eyes. Mrs. Renzulli lifted her hands from the piano keys and smiled broadly. "Beautiful, girls, just beautiful. I hope you will perform that well on the night of the concert."

Dawn could feel pride surge through her. She

had hit the high note and gotten the part without any magic interference. She flashed Megan a thumbs-up sign. She was still impatient for her powers to come back. But it was awfully nice to know that sometimes you could achieve something all on your own.

Mrs. Kronovitch was doing it again. "What is the First Amendment to the Constitution? Dawn? And why is freedom of speech so important, Dawn? Dawn, can you give the class an example of something that might happen without the right to speak freely?" Mrs. Kronovitch's questions were endless.

It had started the day after Dawn dreamed about Albert Einstein materializing in the living room. Dawn had come to Social Studies unprepared. After that, Social Studies class had turned into one huge pop quiz for her.

Dawn knew she'd brought it upon herself. But for the past two days, she'd answered every single one of the teacher's questions correctly. Besides, it had been embarrassing enough just to be caught without her homework assignment. Getting called on every five minutes on top of that wasn't fair. As far as freedom of speech went, Dawn could do with a little more freedom, and a lot less speech.

Social Studies aside, it had been a pretty relaxing few days. It was nice to be just plain Dawn again. Cindy Mitchell had never quite gotten around to reinviting her to the slumber party, but Dawn found she didn't feel as hurt as she might have felt a few weeks ago. She was happy to walk down the halls without being famous. Or hated. And if Jennifer was still a bit distant, at least she wasn't out and out mad. Dawn had her fingers crossed that as soon as she was able to give her cousin a magic demonstration, Jennifer would understand everything. The sooner the better.

So first thing every morning, Dawn checked to see if her magic was back. And then she checked again and again. It was impossible to be patient.

Face it, she told herself, *you miss the excitement.* With the magic, you never knew exactly what would happen next. Being without it was kind of like eating rocky road ice cream without the chips, marshmallows, or nuts.

"Dawn? Would you care to share your thoughts with the rest of us? Or would you care to answer the question?"

Dawn could feel her cheeks turning bright red. She could just imagine sharing her thoughts with the class. *Well, I was sitting here wondering when my magical powers were going to come back.* Instead, she lowered her gaze. "Um, would you mind repeating the question, Mrs. Kronovitch?"

"Oh, so you weren't listening!" Mrs. Kronovitch cried triumphantly.

Dawn looked down at the doodles in her notebook margins. She could feel the stares of everyone in class. "What a bully," she heard Megan say under her breath.

"What was that? Did you have something to say, Megan?" Mrs. Kronovitch had a new focus for her scare tactics.

"Oh, uh, no, Mrs. Kronovitch." Dawn heard the fear in Megan's voice. Now Dawn was starting to get angry. Why did Mrs. Kronovitch have to pick on everyone in class in order to have a good day? A teacher was a person you were supposed to respect. But in this case someone needed to teach the teacher some respect. Dawn's eyebrow twitched with irritation and she did nothing to stop it. Her powers weren't working anyway.

Or were they? Mrs. Kronovitch's steely expression melted right in front of Dawn's eyes. "Well," she said to Megan, "I guess I was hearing things. Now, where was I? Oh, yes. Dawn, I suppose you've answered enough questions today."

Her powers were back! Dawn felt like getting up and dancing on top of her desk. But she had had a little too much attention already this week, so she stayed in her seat.

As Mrs. Kronovitch turned toward the board, Megan leaned across the aisle. "Wow! What happened to *her*?"

Dawn couldn't hold back a huge grin. "I think," she said, "that it must have been magic!"

Ten

"Show and Tell time!" Dawn said. She glanced up and down the empty street, shading her eyes from the afternoon sun. In the distance, a car honked, and music blared from one of the houses across the road. But right here, she and Jennifer were alone.

"Show and tell what? Dawn, don't start getting weird on me again. First you make a big deal about walking home together and then you barely say a word. What's the mystery?"

"I had to get you in private," Dawn said.

"Well, you've got me," Jennifer answered. "Hey, want a stick of gum?" Dawn took a piece and popped it in her mouth. As soon as her teeth closed on it, she knew she'd been had.

"Yuck!" She spit it into her hand. "It's pepper or something!"

Jennifer dissolved in laughter.

Dawn deposited the trick gum in the garbage can in front of the next house they passed. "Jen, I'm trying to be serious." In fact, the joke served to remind her that Jennifer, number one prankster, was about to find out that she could be out-tricked with the raise of an eyebrow.

"If you want to be serious, maybe you've come to the wrong place," Jennifer said. She popped a piece of the pepper gum in her mouth and chomped away. Somehow she had managed to acquire a taste for her own trick.

"Jen, I'm ready to prove it." Dawn tried to steady her nerves, but she'd found out just how awful it was not to have Jennifer's friendship. She couldn't bear for anything to go wrong between them again.

"Prove what?"

"Prove that I'm magic." Dawn and Jennifer made a right onto Bayberry Lane, the Nicholsons' street.

"That again? Are you having a relapse from the

beginning of the week? Dawn, I thought you said you were being serious."

"I am."

"Come on, Dawn. What are you talking about?" Jennifer sounded annoyed.

"I'm talking about making something move without touching it, or turning one thing into something else."

Jennifer dismissed Dawn's words with a wave of her hand. "Come on, Dawn! This is nuts." Then she flashed a smile. "Oh! I see. You're trying to get back at me for the gum." She giggled. "Pretty good one."

"It's not a pretty good one. It's true." Dawn checked once more to make certain they were alone. "I'm magic, Jen, and no one in Crestfield knows it except you and me."

"Dawn, I think you've really lost it. I mean, you might as well tell me it's not a beautiful, sunny day and expect me to believe you."

"Uh-huh." Dawn looked up into the bright blue afternoon. This was it. Ever so slightly, she wiggled her right eyebrow. Instantly, a dark, thick cover of clouds rolled in, turning the sky charcoal gray and blocking out the sun. An unusually cold wind blew down Jennifer's street. "Jen, I hate to tell you this, but it's *not* a beautiful sunny day."

Jennifer's blue eyes registered surprise. She squeezed them shut, then opened them again, as if a second look might bring back the sun.

"Well?" Dawn asked softly. Maybe Jennifer would believe her now.

Jennifer shrugged. "It's a fog. It'll burn off."

"At three-thirty in the afternoon? Besides, where do you think it came from so fast?"

Jennifer looked uncomfortable. She played with the hem of her short, full skirt.

Dawn peered up at the overcast sky. Maybe Jennifer needed a bigger dose of convincing. A brainstorm struck. Well, actually, more like a snow-storm! Jennifer couldn't explain away snow in Crestfield at this time of the year. Dawn waved her arms over her head as she arched her eyebrow. She tried to get a clear picture in her mind of soft, glistening snowflakes. She hoped she was doing this right. Snow in September seemed like a pretty tall order.

She concentrated hard. A few small flakes danced through the air. Then more. Then the sky was white with snow. It certainly looked real. Dawn smiled. She'd done it! Several snow crystals settled on her bare arm and she shivered. It felt real, too. She wiggled her eyebrow, and a navy blue ski parka appeared over her T-shirt.

"Dawn!" Jennifer's frightened cry disrupted the quiet scene. "Dawn, it's snowing!"

"I know. It's okay," Dawn said. "I didn't mean to scare you. I just wanted you to see that I wasn't making up stories."

Jennifer didn't look very reassured. "Dawn, what's happening?" She stared up at the sky.

"Jen, it's just snow." Dawn stuck her tongue out to catch a flake. It was really kind of neat to have a blizzard the first week of school.

"Snow? It's still summer." Jennifer's teeth chattered. "Hey!" she cried, looking over at Dawn. "You've got a ski jacket! Will you please tell me what's going on?" She rubbed her arms to warm herself up.

"Oops. I forgot your jacket. Sorry, Jen." Dawn raised her eyebrow, and Jennifer was wearing a parka that matched her own, but in red to go with her hightops. In place of her skirt, she now had on a pair of stirrup pants.

Jennifer's eyes were wide with amazement. She

ran a hand over her parka to make sure it was real. "Wait a minute!" she said incredulously. "I'm wearing a ski jacket. And it's snowing. Now. In the summer. In Crestfield. That means—" Her sentence hung in the snowy air. She stared at Dawn, then up at the sky, then back at Dawn. She scooped up the thin layer of snow that had fallen on the car parked at the curb. She packed it into a snowball, turning it around and inspecting it. Suddenly she let out a loud cry and let the snowball sail through the air. "Whoa! Dawn, this is amazing!" She jumped up and down.

"The snow?" Dawn cleared some snow from the car's windshield and packed her own snowball. It was icy cold against her bare palms. With a giggle, she hurled it into the sky. It landed softly at her feet. It *was* amazing to be throwing snowballs at the end of summer.

"I mean the snow, your magic, everything!" Jennifer replied, her words coming out as puffs of blue-gray steam in the chilly afternoon air.

"So you're not upset? And you're not going to tell anyone?"

"Are you kidding? This is our absolute best secret!" Jennifer's cheeks were pink with cold and excitement. "We have special powers! I mean, you have special powers! I mean, well, you know what I'm saying."

"Sure. You're saying that I can do magic. That's what I was trying to tell you all along," Dawn said. She felt a surge of relief. Jennifer believed her. And what's more, she was glad about it.

With a whoop of joy, Dawn scooped up another snowball and chased Jennifer the rest of the way down Bayberry Lane.

"Professor Nicholson, I saw it with my very own eyes! Don't you believe me?" Ginger sounded frantic, which wasn't so unusual. Ginger was an expert at getting frantic. When she was cleaning the Nicholsons' house and the vacuum went on the blink, she got frantic. When she was making dinner for Uncle Kenneth and Jennifer, and she overcooked the rice, she got frantic. When she didn't understand her reading assignment for Uncle Kenneth's archaeology class, she got frantic.

Of course, this time Dawn could understand Ginger's feelings. Dawn and Jennifer exchanged glances. They had quietly slipped into the house and were standing just outside Jennifer's father's study. There wasn't a trace of snow left on the ground, and Dawn had made sure their ski jackets were gone. But Ginger had looked outside at just the wrong moment.

Now Ginger was insistent. "I was looking out the window a few minutes ago, and all of a sudden it started to snow. Really it did."

"Ginger," Uncle Kenneth said impatiently, "It's not even fall yet."

"Professor, I saw it!" Ginger cried.

"Ginger, how are you ever going to become a good archaeologist if you can't make accurate observations?" Uncle Kenneth chided. Despite what he was saying now, Dawn knew Uncle Kenneth thought Ginger was one of his best students.

Dawn and Jennifer poked their heads into the study. Dusty books lined the walls and were piled all over the floor. Pieces of broken pottery and ancient tools were everywhere. The paperweight on the desk was some creepy animal skull. "Hi, Ginger. Hi, Uncle Kenneth," Dawn said. "Oh, don't get up." She went over to Uncle Kenneth's desk and gave him a hug. His thick salt-and-pepper beard tickled her cheek.

"What kind of trouble have you girls been getting into?" Uncle Kenneth asked fondly, peering over his round, rimless glasses. "Been playing in any snowstorms? Ginger here thinks she saw one. Right outside."

"A snowstorm?" Dawn asked innocently.

"At this time of the year?" Jennifer asked, just as innocently. "I think you've been making Ginger look at too many old plates and things. It's going to her head," Jennifer said.

The second the girls were up in Jennifer's room with the door closed, they exploded into giggles.

"Snowstorm?" Jennifer mimicked, flopping down on her bed. She kicked her sneakers off and they landed on a pile of not-yet-folded clothing. The shirt she'd worn a few days ago still had the trick flower pinned to it.

"Us, in trouble?" Dawn sputtered, sinking into the rope hammock stretched across the middle of her cousin's cluttered room. Jennifer said that Uncle Kenneth often slept in one just like it when he was out on field trips. Dawn rocked back and forth as her laughter died down. "So. You're really not upset about me? I was really scared."

"Upset? Why? You're going to teach me everything you know, right?" Jennifer replied easily.

Dawn got her first inkling of trouble. "Well, actually Jen, it's not a matter of teaching. I mean, I could explain it all to you in more detail than I already have, but powers are something you're born with." She waited uneasily for Jennifer's reaction.

"You weren't. You went thirteen years being just like me."

"Uh-uh," Dawn said uncomfortably. "They were inside me all along. Only I didn't know it. Remember I told you outside that they don't show up immediately?" She did her best to explain how important it was to be grown up enough to use the powers properly. "The popularity spell was probably something I should have been more careful about."

"Doesn't sound so bad to me," Jennifer mused.

"Well, it was fun," Dawn admitted. "For a while. But, Jen, you're already so popular. What do you need a spell for?"

Jennifer sat up. "Before, when you were telling me what happened to you, you said the teachers fell under the spell too, right? Well, I wouldn't mind it if my average was a little higher this year."

"Then maybe you should study a little harder this year," Dawn said practically.

Jennifer wrinkled her nose. "It'd be so much easier for you to just wiggle your eyebrow."

Dawn bit her lip. "But it would be cheating. I realize that now."

Jennifer was quiet for a moment. "I get it," she said finally. "You don't want to teach me how to do magic, and you won't do it for me. Fine."

"You *are* upset," said Dawn.

"No, I'm not. I said I was excited for you, and I am," Jennifer insisted. "But I sort of assumed you'd share some of your magic with your best friend and favorite cousin."

"Jen, I wish I could teach you to do what I do. But I already explained, either you have it, or you don't."

"We're related. Maybe I have it, too, only I don't know it, either," Jennifer said hopefully.

"Jen, I hate to break it to you, but the power comes from Grandma Cassie's side."

"Oh." Jennifer pouted.

"Jen, I know you think I'm being selfish, but in a way I've already shared some of my magic with you." Dawn said softly. "Remember on my birthday when you were going to dive off that branch?"

"How could I forget? It was amazing that the

branch—" Jennifer stopped short. "That branch! Dawn, you saved me, didn't you?"

Dawn nodded.

For a second, Jennifer was tongue-tied. "I guess I owe you a pretty enormous thank-you."

"Forget it. It's not a matter of thanks. I mean, how could I *not* save my favorite cousin in the whole world? *That's* what my powers are for, you know? So maybe you can understand why I don't feel right about using them to get you in good with the teachers at school?" Dawn held her breath.

"Well . . ." Jennifer paused. "Maybe I'd do it differently if I were you. But I'm not you. Unfortunately."

"Oh, Jen, don't say that. That's how I got in trouble in the first place. Wishing I was more like you."

Jennifer seemed to be thinking this over. Then she let out a short laugh. "Boy, first you're going around trying to be more like me, and now I'm wishing I were more like you. Pretty pointless, huh?"

"Yeah," Dawn agreed. "I wouldn't want you to be anyone but who you are."

"You wouldn't? I was thinking I was going to

seem like the most boring person in the world now that you can do all this neat stuff."

"You? Boring?" It was Dawn's turn to laugh. "No way."

"Really?" Jennifer sounded a little unsure of herself. It wasn't something Dawn was used to hearing.

"Of course not, Jen. You'll never be boring. And anyway, I'm still the same person. And you're still my favorite cousin and best friend. I mean, if you want to be."

Jennifer's confident grin was back. "Shake on it?"

Dawn nodded. Jennifer jumped off the bed, came over to the hammock, and stuck out her hand. Dawn took it in her own.

"Yeow!" A jolt of electricity shot through her fingers. She pulled her arm back. "Jen! You joy-buzzed me!" Jennifer confirmed this by turning her hand over to reveal the offending contraption.

"Hey, you'd better be careful. Now that I have magical powers," joked Dawn, "I can trick you for a change."

"But it would be cheating," Jennifer countered.

"Right. It would be. But this wouldn't." Dawn jumped out of the hammock and grabbed the shirt with the trick flower on it. She pointed the flower at Jennifer and chased her around the room.

"Ooo, now I'm scared," Jennifer yelled with mock terror. She yanked open her night table drawer—the one filled with toys and tricks. Pulling out a water pistol, she launched a counterattack. Sprays of water mingled with peals of laughter.

"If you surrender now, I'll dry this room up in a magical instant!" Dawn giggled.

"Me, surrender? Never!" Jennifer let go another squirt. Dawn's spirits seemed to shoot through the air with it. Jennifer and she were still a team. And their friendship was stronger than magic. Jennifer had proved that. Dawn closed her eyes and made a silent wish.

If it worked as well as her birthday wish, Dawn and Jennifer were going to be best friends for a long, long time.

ABOUT THE AUTHOR

EVE BECKER discovered her own magical powers in eighth grade when she got her teachers to believe her homework excuses. She has been inventing stories ever since. She has lived in Spain and France, but her permanent residence is in New York City with her husband, William Liebeskind, a painter. In her free time, she enjoys sports, dance, and traveling.

Bewitching
new series!

Get ready for teen magic with

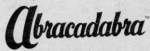

by Eve Becker

ABRACADABRA mixes magic with middle school for an unbeatable new series you'll love! Dawn has always been an ordinary girl. That is, until the summer before eighth grade when Dawn discovers she's inherited magical powers. Only her cousin Jennifer knows the secret—and together the two are going to have their best year yet! Get ready for spells that backfire, mysterious love potions, bewitching fun and more!

☐ 15730-2 THIRTEEN MEANS MAGIC #1 $2.75
☐ 15731-0 THE LOVE POTION #2 $2.75

Skylark is Riding High with Books for Girls Who Love Horses!

Great FREE offer
just for you!

Join SNEAK PEEKS™!

Do you want to know what's new before anyone else? Do you like to read great books about girls just like you? If you do, then you won't want to miss SNEAK PEEKS™! Be the first of your friends to know what's hot ... When you join SNEAK PEEKS™, we'll send you FREE inside information in the mail about the latest books ... *before they're published!* Plus updates on your favorite series, authors, and exciting new stories filled with friendship and fun ... adventure and mystery ... girlfriends and boyfriends.

It's easy to be a member of SNEAK PEEKS™. Just fill out the coupon below ... and get ready for fun! It's FREE! Don't delay—sign up today!